Before Leah realized what was happening James's strong hands circled her waist and she was high in the air. He turned round and round, and Leah felt light as a feather as he lowered her smoothly to his shoulder. Leah's startled thought was, "This is dancing. This is what partnering is all about."

Patrick's voice rose above the passionate Prokofiev music. "Look down into your partner's face now. He's supposed to be your Romeo!"

Leah had anticipated her teacher's orders. Quite naturally she found herself looking down into James's dark, soulful eyes. Suddenly he didn't seem like James at all. The arrogant expression, the haughty, slightly bored look were both gone. He was gazing into her eyes as if he adored her. An unfamiliar thrill coursed up her spine. For a moment Leah wished James could hold her this way forever.

CENTER STAGE

Satin Slippers #2

Elizabeth Bernard

FAWCETT GIRLS ONLY • NEW YORK

RLI: VL 7 & up
       IL 8 & up

A Fawcett Girls Only Book
Published by Ballantine Books
Copyright © 1987 by Cloverdale Press, Inc.

Library of Congress Catalog Card Number: 87-91536

ISBN 0-449-13300-1

Manufactured in the United States of America

First Edition: December 1987

With special thanks to Capezio by Balletmakers and Gilda Mark for Flexitard.

For Janice

I'm in love! fifteen-year-old Leah
Stephenson mused dreamily as she basked in the
warm October sun. She leaned back on her elbows and savored the delicious tingly feeling that
ran straight from the tip of her sneaker-clad feet
to the top of her dancer's bun. She surveyed the
crowd of students milling between the buildings
that made up the San Francisco Ballet Academy.
A steady stream of dancers—mostly girls—traveled
the path between the art studio, its adjacent
bubble-topped swimming pool, and the Victorian
mansion that housed the main portion of the
prestigious dance school.

Leah sighed and closed her eyes, hardly able to
believe how lucky she was. She had never imagined she would feel so passionately about a
place before coming to SFBA. But here she was,
totally, hopelessly, head-over-heels in love with
her new school: the buildings, the teachers, the

1

rigorous dance curriculum, the new friends she had made. Everything about it was absolutely perfect, like a dream come true.

Leah lay back on the freshly mowed lawn and enjoyed a rare moment of quiet between the morning and afternoon sessions. A textbook was resting on her knees and its glossy pages flapped gently in the light breeze that blew in from the bay. Leah's mind was about a million miles away from her book. She was thinking about that morning's class with Madame Preston.

During adagio exercises, the teacher, who was also the director of the school, told Leah that she had a port de bras that was as soft and expressive as the great English-born ballerina, Alicia Markova. Remembering the compliment, Leah's generous mouth widened into a smile. Keeping her face toward the sun, and her eyes closed, she gracefully lifted her arms into a low fifth position, then opened them wide into second.

"Is that some new way of doing math homework?" Alexandra Sorokin asked in a throaty voice.

Leah's eyes popped open and she quickly sat up. Her friend Alex was stretched out on the grass beside her. Her dark almond-shaped eyes peered at Leah over the cover of the thick novel she was reading. Leah couldn't see Alex's mouth, but she could tell from her eyes she was laughing.

"Uh—no." She giggled in embarrassment. "Just fixing my hair," she joked. She reached up and pulled the pins out of her topknot, letting her blond hair cascade thick and shimmering down to her waist.

Alex put her book down and playfully shook a warning finger in Leah's face. "Don't you have a geometry test tomorrow?"

Leah looked glum. "Don't remind me." She combed her fingers through her tangled waves and moaned. "If I could only *dance* my way through that stupid test, I'd be okay."

Then she flopped down again and propped her feet up on the arms of a white wooden lawn chair. She tossed her book onto the ground and kicked off her sneakers. Pink tights peeked from beneath her purple overalls and blades of grass stuck to the sleeves and back of her black leotard.

Alex arched one eyebrow and regarded Leah with an amused expression on her high-cheek-boned face. "But you can't dance your way through a school examination," she said in a matter-of-fact voice. "Besides, geometry isn't that hard." She gave a dismissive wave of her hand.

Leah sniffed in protest. "That's easy for you to say, Sorokin. You didn't have geometry with Mr. Creighton. And anyway," she added, tossing a handful of cut grass at her friend, "not all of us are brainy math whizzes."

Alex regally brushed the grass off her black turtleneck sweater and repeated in a puzzled tone, "Whizzes?"

Leah tried not to laugh. Alexandra had been born in Russia and had been living in America only a few years. She had landed at SFBA after her famous dancer parents had defected from the Soviet Union and come to the States. The Russian girl's English was good, but Leah's self-appointed task since coming to the school was to help Alex master the nuances of American slang.

"Whizzes. . . ." Leah searched her mind for a simple explanation. After a moment her large blue eyes lit up. "You know, someone who's good at something."

Alex nodded. "I see. You're a whiz at pirouettes. I'm a whiz at mathematics. We're both whizzes at wasting time!" Her dark eyes glinted with mischief as she stretched out her leg and kicked Leah's book back toward her. "You, too, would be a whiz at geometry if you worked on it half as hard as you work on your dancing," she pointed out in a superior voice.

Leah just groaned. Ignoring the book, she squinted through half-closed eyes up at the cloudless sky and mused aloud. "Back at San Lorenzo High, no one expected me to be as good at math as I was at dancing. All my teachers knew I wanted to be a dancer and I didn't have time for a lot of schoolwork. Here," Leah continued in an exasperated tone, "I not only have to dance my best for four hours a day, I also have to pull at least a C average to stay in. It's not fair."

"Well, if you're not happy here, no one said you have to stay," Alex teased.

Leah glared at her friend in mock disgust. She sat up straight and hugged her knees to her chest, then turned toward Alex. She brushed a wisp of hair back from her face and grinned. "Are you kidding? I've never been so happy in my whole life. I *love* it here!" she declared exuberantly. She pinched her wrist, hard, just as she had at least

once each day since she had been accepted
at SFBA. She wanted to make sure this past
month was real. Alexandra returned her smile,
then went back to her book.

When Leah had decided to become a professional dancer, her mother had warned her that
choosing a career at so young an age would rob
her of a normal high school life. The thought
made Leah smile. As far as she was concerned,
nothing about San Lorenzo had been normal for
her anyway. Life at the San Francisco Ballet Academy might not be "normal" for most kids, but
Leah felt as if she were someplace she really
belonged, someplace where her passion for dance
wasn't considered unusual, where no one thought
her dreams of being a great ballerina were so
farfetched.

She propped her chin in her hands and watched
a group of girls saunter by. Leah knew they weren't
talking about baseball or the junior prom or who
was dating whom. They were probably talking
about dancing, gossiping about members of the
Bay Area Ballet company, who said what to whom
in class, who would get the roles in the upcoming
school performances. These were the subjects of
most of the conversations Leah found herself involved in with the two really good friends she
had made since arriving in San Francisco, Alexandra Sorokin and Kay Larkin. They all lived together at Mrs. Hanson's boardinghouse not far
from the school and Leah already found it hard to
imagine what life would be like without them,

or—though she missed her mother—living back home again.

With a determined gesture she reached for her book. No, nothing, not even having to study hard for geometry, would tempt her to go back to her old life in San Lorenzo, California, and her regimen of just one daily ballet class after school at the Hannah Greene School of Dance and Theatre Arts. Here Leah got to dance almost all day long: morning class at 9 A.M. with Madame Preston; schoolwork between eleven and one; then pas de deux class, character sessions, modern, repertory, or choreography, depending on which day it was. Leah had never worked so hard in her life, but she loved every minute of it. And if staying at SFBA meant keeping at least a C average, then Leah would manage it. As Alex had said, if she worked as hard at geometry as she did on her pirouettes, she'd get by.

Leah opened her book to a page full of dreaded illustrations of isosceles, equilateral, and scalene triangles. She allowed herself one last look at the glimmering bay spread out below, then with a soft sigh began memorizing the day's lesson.

"Leah! Alex! *There* you are." Kay Larkin's merry voice floated over the lawn toward the two girls.

Leah looked up. Kay's dark curly head was poking out of the open window of the Academy's office, where she worked a couple of hours a week on a partial work-study scholarship. She waved an envelope in Leah's direction. Leah waved back and beckoned for Kay to join her and Alex. Kay ducked her head inside and a moment later she bounded across the yard, pulled up a saggy plastic lounge chair, and sank down breathlessly.

"You aren't going to believe this!" she announced, handing Leah the envelope. "I've got the most incredible news." She turned her dark blue eyes from Leah to Alex and back to Leah again and bounced up and down on the edge of her seat.

"Have you sneaked a peek at Leah's mail?" Alexandra accused, feigning horror.

Kay flashed her a withering look. "Of course not," she protested, planting her hands on her hips. "If that's the kind of friend you think I am, well, I just won't let you in on my latest bit of Academy gossip." She pouted and began to get up.

Leah looked up from her letters. "Gossip?" She looked at Kay and raised her eyebrows. "Did I hear the magic word?"

Alex nodded. "I heard it, too. Isn't it funny" —she leaned back on one elbow and buffed her fingernails against the sleeve of her sweater— "how a person who has been here less than one month seems to know so much more about what is going on than a person like me who's been here for two entire years."

"If you're going to make fun of me ..." Kay warned, fighting to keep a smile off her face.

Leah cracked up. "We aren't making fun of you for being a walking grapevine. We're just jealous. No one ever tells me their juiciest secrets." Kay amazed Leah. Over the past three and a half weeks the petite curly-haired dancer had affec-

tionately wound her way into the hearts of everybody at the Academy. Even stern Madame Preston
seemed less than absolutely strict with Kay in
spite of her carefree attitude and less than con-
sistent performance in the girls' daily morning
class. Somehow Kay's friendly, open nature led
other people, staff and students alike, to confide
in her, to tell her all sorts of savory news bulle-
tins about the Bay Area Ballet company and the
school.

"Of course, by the time she tells us, it will be
old news," Alex remarked pointedly, feigning a
yawn.

Kay smirked happily. With deliberate slow-
ness she rummaged in her bag and pulled out a
mirror. She dabbed some blush on her already
pink cheeks and glanced at Leah. She grinned like
a cat, then leaned back in the chair and said
apologetically, "But then, I'm acting like I'm the
only one with news. Who's your letter from?"

"From my best friend at home, Chrissy Morley,
as I'm sure you've noticed already." She tapped
the corner of the envelope where the return address was written with several different colored
pens.

"Aren't you going to read it to us?" Kay continued her game of making her friends wait. She
settled back in her chair and regarded Leah with
wide innocent eyes.

Leah's answer was quick and sweet. "I might—
depending on how exciting that news of yours
really is." Both Alex and Kay looked forward to
Chrissy's long, newsy weekly letter to Leah. Alex-

andra loved hearing what she called a blow-by-blow description of American high school life and Kay said Chrissy's letters made her less homesick herself.

"Kay ..." Alex reached out and shook Kay's foot. "We're sorry. We're dying to hear your news. Please tell us."

"Now that you asked politely, maybe I will!" Kay retorted, then jumped excitedly to her feet. "In a few weeks we—at least some of us—" she corrected herself, "are going to perform on a real live stage, with dancers from the Bay Area Ballet."

Leah couldn't believe her ears. "You mean that?"

Alex looked less than impressed. "What kind of stage?"

Kay glared at Alex and explained with exaggerated patience. "Alex, I'm sure you've seen one or two in your day. You know, a place with spotlights, footlights, floorboards. We get to wear makeup. There's a real audience." She turned to Leah and continued enthusiastically, ignoring Alexandra's skeptical reaction. "I was helping with the filing in the office, and I couldn't help but overhear Patrick on the phone with someone from the California Council for the Arts. It turns out that students from the Academy are going to take part in a series of dance lectures and demonstrations at local high schools, and company members will be part of the show, too. I'm *so* excited."

"So that's all." Alexandra was visibly disappointed. "That happens every year. I've taken part in it ever since I got here, and let me tell you, it's a lot of work. All these kids you dance in front of just blow bubble gum and talk and giggle and the boys whistle." Her full mouth curved down with distaste. "They don't seem too interested in ballet." She gave a disgusted toss of her head and eyed the thick envelope in Leah's hand eagerly. Chrissy's news obviously appealed to her more than Kay's.

Leah sat back on her heels and sighed dreamily. Maybe dancing in front of a bunch of high school kids wasn't as big a deal as dancing on the stage of a real theater, but it was a beginning. "Oh, Kay, it's wonderful news. I can't wait. Who's going to be picked? Will everyone get a chance to perform? Even first-year students? And what are we dancing? " She shot her questions rapid-fire at Kay.

Kay let out a lovely laugh and shielded her face with her hands as if to ward off Leah's enthusiasm. "I don't have *all* the answers yet! Give me a chance." She looked around, then lowered her voice and beckoned the two other girls closer. "I do know one thing, though. I heard Patrick, Diana, and that really cute new teacher, Evan Macaulay, talking it over: students—not company members— are going to be chosen to dance the balcony scene from *Romeo and Juliet*!"

Alexandra screeched. She grabbed Kay's arm and shook her fiercely. "Are you sure about that?"

Kay nodded and looked smug. She had just made Alexandra Sorokin lose her cool, and that was pretty big news in itself. She sat back happily and related what she had overheard the teachers discussing. "They felt it would be fun for the audience to have kids their own age dancing a ballet about teenagers," she said in conclusion.

"Dancing Juliet would be so—so—" Alex looked eagerly from Leah to Kay and tried to find the right words. "It would be so perfect." She let out a long, wistful sigh. "Last year when the company premiered the new production of *Romeo* at the Opera House, all I wanted to do was dance Juliet. I memorized every single step. I don't care whom I get to dance it in front of, or with, or anything." Alex cut herself off, and looked embarrassed at her outburst. She sat up straight and brushed a speck of dust off her black stretch pants. "Well, that certainly is big news and I can't wait until the auditions."

"Auditions?" Kay and Leah exclaimed in unison.

Alex gave a puzzled frown. "Well, of course. That's how they always pick roles around here. It's part of a dancer's training." In spite of her Russian accent, she did a fairly good imitation of Madame Preston's cultured voice.

Kay looked skeptical. "But Patrick said they want to give lots of new students a chance to dance."

"Oh, they will. These dance demonstrations go on for months, through the whole school year. They put together a program and groups tour the schools. They'll probably have first and second and third casts. It is a good chance to perform, I guess. But I wouldn't even try out at this point if it weren't for *Romeo and Juliet.*"

"I can't imagine anyone picking me for Juliet,"

Kay said, unable to mask the disappointment in her voice.

"Oh, I wouldn't say that," Alex responded. "Besides, there will be other parts. I'm sure they already have you in mind to perform some of those allegro steps you're such a—such a whiz at." She looked toward Leah to make sure she had used the word correctly.

Leah nodded, looking thoughtful. "That's probably right, but to be honest"—Leah met Alex's eyes and didn't flinch as she said, "I know I'd give anything to dance Juliet too. Everyone's going to feel like that." There wasn't a challenge in her voice, just a simple statement of fact, but Kay got her drift instantly.

The tiny dancer let out a sigh. "We're always going to be competing for parts around here. I guess we'd better get used to it."

"That's not absolutely true," Alex said slowly. "We're different types, so we won't compete all that much, though in a case like this, type isn't as important. It depends on the guys who are ready to dance *Romeo*."

"I hadn't thought of that!" Leah gasped. She couldn't think of *one* new boy who would make a very good Romeo.

"I didn't hang around long enough to hear anything about the boys," Kay wailed. "Patrick and Diana were still talking about the girls when I left."

"We'll find out soon enough. And anyway, *we're* not just competing among ourselves," Alex said. "As Leah said, everyone is going to have their heart set on that one pas de deux. And it won't just be first-year students jumping into the act. Unfortunately, not everyone will get to dance it. But I know I'm going to try my best to get that part."

"Me, too," Leah said promptly, shredding some grass with her hand. Out of the corner of her eye she glanced at Kay, then at Alex. Depending on the Romeo the powers-that-be in the school had in mind, Kay just might have an outside chance. But she was so tiny, few of the boys looked right dancing with her. Alex was another story. She was tall, but not too tall, and very beautiful in a dark way that would be perfect for the Italian heroine of a Shakespeare play. If she were a judge, she'd pick Alex over any other girl in the school. She was an accomplished dancer, more advanced than Leah, and she had more experience than most of the students, especially with partnering. Alexandra was the only student besides Leah to hold the coveted Golden Gate Award, a four-year scholarship given only occasionally to a particularly promising new student. Other girls would be trying out for the part, but Leah was sure the battle lines would be drawn between her and Alex and maybe just one or two other students. The thought wasn't a pleasant one. "I just hope it doesn't get in the way of friendship," she said in a low voice, almost to herself.

But Alex heard her. "It won't. It doesn't have to," the Russian girl said firmly, scrambling to her feet.

Leah wasn't convinced. She was going to feel

pretty crummy if Alex or Kay got the coveted part. And it was hard picturing proud Alexandra Sorokin not reacting if one of her friends topped her performance at the audition.

Chapter 2

"AHHHHH—!" James Cummings's anguished cry echoed through the Red Studio. The next sound was a terrible thump as he dropped Pamela Hunter in the middle of the floor. She landed hard on her rear, open-mouthed and dazed, looking up at her partner, her surprised green eyes watering with pain. The pianist stopped the accompaniment mid-chord and the pas de deux class came to a halt.

"What are you doing, Cummings?" Patrick Hogan shouted from the front of the room. The sandy-haired teacher jumped off his chair and hurried to Pamela's side.

As he brushed by, Leah pressed herself back against the barre and held her breath. The usually mild-mannered Bay Area Ballet principal was red-faced, and as he passed by she thought she could actually feel the anger radiating out of him like heat from the sun.

Under her breath she murmured to Alex, "James is really going to get it now." Pam wasn't Leah's favorite person at the school—not by a long shot—but at the moment Leah felt sorry for her.

"Don't kid yourself!" Alex scoffed softly, bending over to retie the satin ribbons on her toe shoes. When she straightened up again she had her old-hand-at-SFBA look in her eye. She leaned closer to Leah and continued. "James never gets in trouble. Haven't you noticed that around here boy dancers—with even a hint of talent—can do no wrong. James Cummings has more than a hint of talent. No matter what you think of him, you have to admit that. Everyone treats him with kid gloves. Besides, probably whatever happened just now is not his fault."

How could dropping a partner like that not be a boy's fault? Leah wondered, but she didn't bother to argue with Alex. When it came to James, Alex was absolutely blind. For reasons Leah couldn't possibly fathom, Alex considered the haughty boy one of her best friends at the school. At first Leah had been sure Alex had a crush on the good-looking dancer, but Alex had assured Leah she wasn't interested in James that way. She just liked talking to him, and more than that, dancing with him. Being partnered by James, Alex swore, was to experience exactly what dancing was all about.

It was an experience Leah was quite sure she could live without.

Alex elbowed Leah gently in the ribs. "Here comes the fun part!"

Leah followed Alex's gaze. Patrick was helping Pam to her feet. "Are you hurt?" he asked.

Pam blinked back her tears and shook her head. "I don't think so," she answered, her voice a bit shaky. She started to walk around in a tight little circle, massaging the small of her back with one fist. With the other hand she jabbed strands of her thick red hair back into her bun. Her nails were long and polished a deep red. She winced each time she stepped on her right foot, and she leaned on Patrick's arm while she worked her ankle up and down. Patrick watched her carefully and a worried expression crossed his kind face. "Maybe you'd better sit out the rest of the class."

His words had a strong effect on Pam. She pulled her hand from his shoulder and with a proud toss of her head declared, "I'm fine. Just fine." She looked around the room. When she spotted James, an angry blush started up her pale back and neck. A moment go her eyes had been bright with tears; now they were ablaze with rage. She whirled around and faced Patrick. Her voice was hard and steady as a rock. "I'm fine. I didn't get hurt. But I could have been. If he ever does that again, I'll—I'll—"

"You'll do what?" James stomped across the floor and planted himself very close to Pam. He glared down at her in silence for a moment, then whipped the towel from his hand and displayed his palm to Patrick. Even from where she stood, Leah could see the ugly red gash. James hadn't been faking it after all. Leah's pity for Pam began fading fast. "Look, look what she did," James complained bitterly. "It's those daggers that little witch calls nails. Believe me, Patrick, I won't dance with her again. *Ever*." He punctuated his last remark with a stamp of his foot, and after giving Pam a scathing look, paraded away to the opposite side of the room. He folded his arms across his chest and began to sulk.

Alex grabbed Leah's arm and squeezed hard. Leah glanced at her in confusion, then suddenly realized why Alex looked expectant, hopeful, happier than she had since Patrick had made everyone change partners a few days ago. Alex had landed with a new boy named Tim Cortez and Pam had been paired with James. Now, if James refused to dance with Pam, maybe Alex could go back to working with him again.

Leah pressed Alex's hand for luck and to show that she understood.

Patrick had taken James aside. Leah watched for a moment as they talked. James's expression darkened with every word, and Leah figured Patrick was trying to talk him into dancing with Pam. She wished the teacher would just give in to the stubborn boy. It would save everybody lots of time and trouble. For a moment James caught her looking at him. His expression didn't change, but there was a flicker of interest in his deep dark eyes, as if he had just noticed something about her. Leah self-consciously put her hand to her hair, then smoothed the back of her filmy practice skirt and blushed. She hated being stared at like that. She drew herself up very tall and abruptly turned away. That boy is so rude, she thought.

With great deliberation she pulled up her leg warmers and faced the barre. She could still see James's and Patrick's reflection in the mirror, but she forced her gaze past them to the large sunlit windows lining the far wall of the studio and very carefully began doing pliés, trying to keep her muscles warm until her time came to dance.

With a sharp clap of his hands Patrick silenced the low murmur in the room. Leah stopped her series of pliés and glanced up. Patrick was back by the piano. He hoisted himself up on the tall stool nestled in the curve of the baby grand and cleared his throat. "Let's take it from the top one more time. First group please. The big diagonal run into a shoulder lift."

Leah let out an impatient sigh as Pamela, Kay, and Katrina Gray took their places in the middle of the room. Would group two ever get their chance? She looked across the studio at her partner of the day. Michael Litvak was stretching his long skinny legs at the barre. He caught Leah's reflection in the mirror and gave her a little wave. Leah smiled back halfheartedly. Michael was sweet, but dancing with him wasn't very much fun. He was so nervous he made Leah feel as if she were about to fall every time he lifted her even a foot off the ground, and he was so tall, sitting on top of his shoulder felt like sitting on top of a skyscraper.

"Leah," Patrick said with the barest hint of a smile. "Change places with Pamela."

Leah's chin jutted forward in surprise, but she

obeyed promptly. Or tried to. Pam stayed glued to her spot.

"I thought *I* was dancing with James!" Pam's voice oozed defiance.

Leah looked quickly at James, but he wasn't looking at her at all. He looked very bored and above it all. His mind was made up about who he intended *not* to dance with and he wasn't going to let anything else faze him. His eyes were closed and he was massaging a spot on his right shoulder. He had apparently forgotten about his wounded hand. The idea of dancing with him didn't appeal to Leah at all. Fleetingly, Leah hoped Patrick would give in to Pam.

He didn't. He clasped his hands behind his back and stared down the angry southern girl. "We're changing partners again. That is"—he added with exaggerated politeness—"if it's okay with you." He paused and added in a slow, deliberate voice. "In fact, until you cut those nails, I'd suggest you sit out pas de deux class. And this goes for all you girls—long nails are dangerous when you're dancing."

No one uttered a word.

Pam drew her breath in sharply. She narrowed her eyes to two green slits and glowered at Leah. When she let out her breath again it sounded to Leah very much like a hiss. Then she turned on her heel and marched to the barre with her head held high. She yanked a shawl out of her dance bag and sat down on the floor.

Leah didn't look in Pam's direction but she could feel her eyes boring holes in her back. Leah fought down a moment's fear. Pam and she had already had one serious run-in since arriving at SFBA. At the moment they weren't even talking, though they lived at the same boardinghouse. When Leah had first come to SFBA to audition, she had struck up an instant friendship with Pam. She was one of the most dynamic, strong-willed people Leah had ever met. But the strain of audition week had bared Pam's true colors: she had outwardly befriended Leah while plotting to steal her special solo variation for the entrance exam. Both girls had been among the handful of new students accepted into the academy. Leah's joy at attending SFBA was some what diminished by the realization that before school even opened she had made an enemy, one who was going to make life pretty unpleasant over the next three or four years. Patrick ordering her to dance with James would be just one more painful thorn in Pamela's side, and Leah didn't relish that thought one bit.

Leah was still worrying about Pam when the music started. She barely had time to lift her arms and point her foot before the cue to begin the fast run into James's arms. Before she realized what was happening, his strong hands circled her waist and she was high in the air. He turned around and around, and Leah felt as light as a feather as he lowered her smoothly to his shoulder. Leah's startled thought was "This is dancing. This is what partnering is all about." Suddenly she knew exactly why Alex loved dancing with James.

Patrick's voice rose above the passionate Prokofiev music. "Look down into your partner's face
now. He's supposed to be your Romeo!"

Leah had anticipated the teacher's orders. Quite
naturally she found herself looking down into
James's dark, soulful eyes, a puzzled expression
on her face. Suddenly he didn't seem like James
at all. The arrogant expression, the haughtly,
slightly bored look were both gone. He was gazing into her eyes as if he adored her. An unfamiliar thrill coursed up her spine. For a moment she
wished James could hold her this way forever.

They were still gazing at each other when the
music stopped. For Leah the room, Pamela, and
all the other kids had disappeared. Kay's giggle
broke the spell. Leah's face grew hot as James
lowered her expertly to the floor. She stepped
away from him quickly. She was cold where his
hands had been around her waist. Her transpar-
ent skirt clung awkwardly to the back of her legs,
and she tugged it down, feeling very self-conscious.
She felt as if she had just shared such an intense
private moment with James, and so many kids
had been watching. She wondered if they had
noticed how he—how she—had just changed, how
something so important had just happened between them.

She cast a quick curious glance up at his face,
but James didn't look like Romeo anymore. He
looked a little bored again, though when he met
her eyes, he granted her a quick, dimpled smile.
"That went well," he said coolly. "I like dancing
with you. Let's hope the boss lets us dance to-

gether again." He gestured with his shoulder toward Patrick, then stretched his arms and turned his back on Leah and began a series of slow, graceful neck rolls.

Leah blinked. She wasn't sure the partner she had just danced with actually existed. Gallant, adoring Romeo had turned back into remote, self-absorbed James.

"That was very good, Leah, James," Patrick said, chewing thoughtfully on a pencil. Leah met the teacher's eye and gave a shy smile. Since she had come to SFBA she had found Patrick to be one of the most sympathetic members of the Academy staff. Any praise from him bolstered Leah's ego for days.

"In fact"—Patrick strode over to Leah and looked her up and down as if seeing her for the first time,—"I'd say you two were just right for each other. I'd like you to work together regularly from here on in." Then to himself he added, "I don't know why I didn't think of that before."

His voice was soft but Leah heard him. Apparently, so did Pam. She scrambled to her feet and frowned at Leah, then snickered slightly. Leah wanted to kick herself. She hated when she let Pam get to her. She tried to remind herself that getting James as a partner was something of a coup. She hoped she looked happier about it than she felt.

"That's enough for today, class," Patrick announced. "I expect you all to go to the library and listen to the tapes of the Prokofiev score for *Romeo and Juliet*—specifically the balcony scene pas de deux now that you've finished learning it. In case you haven't heard via the Academy grapevine"—his eyes rested meaningfully on Kay, who put her hand to her mouth and stifled a laugh—"we're going to be holding auditions the middle of this week for several parts to be danced by students in this year's series of dance lecture/ demonstrations in area high schools. The biggest student piece will be that balcony scene—so get to work and learn it. The first demonstration is scheduled for late next week. That doesn't leave much time for rehearsals. So do your homework. I hope you all choose to try out."

A ripple of excited comments went around the studio. Then everyone remembered that class was over and broke into the traditional applause for their teacher.

As soon as the clapping died down, Leah thoughtfully ambled across the floor to fetch her dance bag from under the piano. The prospect of working regularly with one partner, especially James, should thrill her. But it didn't. Leah's experience with partners was pretty limited. Until coming to SFBA, she had never danced with a boy. Her good jump and strong sense of rhythm had made her a quick study, however, and the first lesson she had learned was that rehearsing a pas de deux with a partner meant plenty of hard work and cooperation. James Cummings didn't promise to be the cooperative type.

"Isn't it great, Leah?" Kay skipped up and gave Leah a quick hug. "You actually get to dance with James, and Pam doesn't!"

Leah shouldered her bright blue carryall and smiled nervously. "Yeah, it is great." She instinctively sought Alex's eyes. Alex knew James so well. Maybe she'd have some advice on how to work with him. When she spotted Alex's face, her heart stopped.

Alex looked hurt. "Oh, Alex!" Leah cried. "I don't want to dance with James. Really I don't." It was true. As great as dancing with James had been, working with him was sure to be a miserable experience. Especially if Alex would be hurting.

Alex raised a hand in warning. She gave a meaningful look around the room. "The walls here have ears," she said cryptically, then flashed Leah a brave smile. "Dancing with James is a very good thing. I'll miss him as a partner, but I think Patrick made up his mind—even before this afternoon—that James and I aren't right for each other." There was a note of disappointment in her voice, and Leah looked down at her feet not knowing what to say. Some instinct told her Patrick was right. James and Alex were too alike to be good partners for each other. They shared the same dark romantic looks and had a similar languid quality to their movement. And Alex was a little tall for James. Someone Leah's height and with brighter coloring—like Pam—would be a better, more attractive partner for the school's star male dancer.

"Besides," Alex went on as the three girls proceeded to the dressing room, "as Kay pointed out, at least he won't be dancing with Pam. And I wouldn't wish Pam on any of my friends." After a moment she gave Leah's shoulder a friendly poke. Though she still looked disappointed, there was no trace of jealousy in her eyes. Leah breathed a sigh of relief.

"Did it feel as good dancing with him as it looked?" Alex's eyes were twinkling now.

"Why? How did it look?" Leah asked innocently.

Kay burst out laughing. "Like Romeo and Juliet." She stopped in her tracks and stared at Leah. "You two would look great dancing that pas de deux in the demonstration." Kay continued toward the dressing room, the bounce gone out of her step. "It's enough to make me not even bother to audition."

Chapter 3

"*Alex, what's James really like?*"
Leah asked two days later, hooking her thumbs in
the straps of her flowered pink suspender pants.
The girls were heading down the second floor
hall toward the changing room. Auditions for the
demonstration program were scheduled to begin
within the hour, but Leah couldn't believe how
calm she felt, calm enough to ask Alex the question that had been on her mind ever since Patrick
decided she and James Cummings would make
perfect partners. She had danced with him twice
since and both times were pure magic—until the
music stopped.

"Why do you ask me that?" Alex sounded
guarded and a little distant. Leah bit her lip. Was
Alex upset about losing James as a partner? She
decided to drop the subject, but Alex was looking
at her intently, waiting for her to answer.

Alex's frank scrutiny was unnerving and Leah

ran her finger around the V-neck of her white cotton T-shirt before replying. Finally she dropped her eyes and stammered, "Uh—well, I don't know. He's a funny guy. When I dance with him, he's one person. As soon as the music stops—"

Alex interrupted with a laugh. "Oh, that!" She smoothed her sleek dark hair back from her face. "James is just that way. When he dances, that's all that exists for him. When he's not dancing, it's like half of him is missing. That's all."

Leah gave Alex a puzzled look. Alex went on to explain. "Don't you see, Leah, he's got the makings of a really *great* dancer."

"You mean the ego!" Leah noted sharply.

"That, too. But even more. He's the most single-minded, determined boy I've ever met. Nothing, and no one, will ever get in the way of his dancing," Alex declared with a fierceness that scared Leah. At the same time, it made her more interested in James.

Alex continued. "You don't meet many dancers—many people—like that." They had come to the end of the hall and Alex stopped and stared thoughtfully out over the lawn. "Yes," she went on more to herself. "That's why I like him so much. He doesn't *have* to work as hard as he does. Dancing comes so naturally to him—like breathing. But he wants to be the best and I respect that. He's very honest that way."

Leah knew honesty was a trait Alex valued more than any other in her friends. Still, she wished the warmth and magic she felt dancing with James would last just a few minutes after their dance was ended.

Alex snapped her fingers in front of Leah's eyes and laughed. "Don't look so worried. Wait until you know him better," she advised. "Give him a chance. Dancing means so much to him, he's a little behind on knowing how to act with people when they aren't dancing with him. He's not a bad person, though," Alex promised. "You'll like him!"

Leah wasn't convinced, just as she wasn't convinced that her question about James had really been answered. She knew he loved to dance and she knew he possessed exceptional talent. She had heard whispered comparisons of James with internationally famous male ballet stars of the present and past like Dowell, Bruhn, and Baryshnikov. Just seeing him once in class during audition week had convinced her he was destined to be a great dancer. But she wondered exactly why having such promise excused him from being civil to his fellow students and partner.

Leah shoved her dance bag farther up her shoulder and looked at a wall clock. "Whoops, we'd better get moving," she commented, then, knowing she'd probably get no better explanation of James's weird behavior from Alex, she changed the subject to the item on the mind of every girl auditioning.

"Hey," she began, "who do you think will get to dance Romeo? I haven't heard a thing about boys' tryouts."

Alex hadn't either.

"My theory," Leah went on, trailing her finger along the top of the polished wainscoting as they hurried toward the dressing room, "is that Juliet will be picked first. Then whoever dances best with her will be Romeo."

Alex greeted Leah's theory with skepticism. "Well, there are only two or three boys who aren't company apprentices who are good enough to dance Romeo." Alex ticked off their names on her fingers. "James, of course. Then my next choice would be Michael Litvak ..."

Leah wrinkled her nose at the idea of her former beanstalk of a partner being Romeo. "He's too tall and not very cute," she complained.

Alex shrugged. "Cute isn't the point. He's a really good dancer, and he may not be polished yet, but we are supposed to be students dancing for students. The Kentwood High School auditorium is scarcely the Opera House!"

"I guess," Leah agreed with a reluctant sigh.

"Then last but not least, Kenny Rotolo."

"Kenny?" Leah repeated, surprised. Then she broke into a wide grin and clapped her hands together. "If Kenny is really in the running, that gives Kay a chance. Only she and Katrina are small enough to dance with Kenny."

Alex stopped a few feet from the dressing room and considered Leah carefully. "Leah, sometimes I don't understand you." She shook her head as if trying to make sense out of something. "You really want Kay to have a fair chance to get the part even though you want it yourself, don't you? I haven't met many people in the dance world as generous as you."

Leah averted her eyes. She didn't feel she really

deserved Alex's compliment. She wanted the part more than anything in the world. Hoping her two best friends at the school would have a fair chance to get it didn't change that feeling. "Stop it, Alex," she finally protested. "I'll die if you or Kay are picked for Juliet. I'll feel just as bad as anyone else around here."

"But you'll still be our friend, and—" Alex started to say, but at the sound of Pamela Hunter's voice, she broke off.

The dressing room door was ajar and Pamela's silky drawl floated out into the hall. As if one mind, Leah and Alex instinctively stopped in their tracks. Leah knew she should just walk in and not eavesdrop. But something kept her rooted to the spot.

"I don't know why we're even bothering to go through the motions of this dumb audition." Pamela's voice dripped sarcasm. "Everyone, and you all better believe *everyone,* knows exactly who is going to get the big part."

"Who?" Katrina's voice asked from behind the half-opened door.

"James's partner, that's who," Pamela sneered in reply. "He's the only student good enough to dance Romeo's solo. Just think about it." A murmur of agreement trickled out the door. Then Pam continued. "A certain blonde around here was smart enough to figure that out fast!" She paused, then delivered her final verdict. "That's why Leah stole him from Alexandra."

"What?" Leah gasped out loud. She flung the door open wide and came face-to-face with a startled Pam. "Why don't you run that by me one more time?" she demanded. It was the first thing she had said to Pam in a month.

"Leah," Alex warned under her breath as she followed into the brightly lit changing room. "The audition is in a few minutes. Don't get yourself all worked up. She's not worth it." Alex brushed by Leah and deposited her dance bag on the nearest available chair. She turned her back on the other girls and began peeling off her clothes.

Pam glowered at Leah from her spot in the corner, and for the moment chose to ignore her challenge. "Some of us aren't very decent. Maybe someone should close the door—tight. You never can tell who's hanging around these halls." She gave Leah another pointed glance, then faced the other way as she slithered into her glossy black leotard.

Without turning around Leah slammed the door behind her. She pressed her back against it and waited for Pamela to repeat her accusation. She looked around the room. The other girls—Katrina, Linda Howe, Mary Ellen Wade—avoided meeting her eye. Pam's friends, Mindy Chalker and Abigail Handhardt looked downright hostile. Leah shook her head in disgust and finally moved away from the door. Pam's one-girl campaign against Leah was having its desired effect. Leah dumped the contents of her bag on the floor in front of the one empty chair and sat down. As she began to undress, she kept her eyes on Pam.

Pamela straightened up and shook out her abundant red hair. She wielded a pink plastic brush in one hand. As she yanked the bristles through the waves, they bounced luxuriously against her face and down her back. How could anyone so beautiful be so nasty, Leah wondered, trying to reconcile the way Pam looked with how she acted.

A little voice inside Leah warned her to keep her mouth shut, that if there was such a thing as a good time to confront Pam, this wasn't it. But Leah was too angry now to listen to her conscience or Alex's advice. Accusing her of stealing James from Alex was the last straw. "What exactly did you mean, Pam, by saying I 'stole' James from Alex? Wasn't he *your* partner last?" Leah said, amazed at how much in control she sounded. Her heart was pounding with anger.

Pam whirled around to face Leah. She looked positively gleeful as she met Leah's challenge. "Patrick had paired me with James just because I'm a better size for him than Alex, that's all." Pam's statement was innocent enough, but the way she said it made Leah's blood boil. She seemed to be insinuating that Alex was too big, or too fat, or something ridiculous like that.

Leah leapt to her friend's defense. "Alex and James worked well together. I think Patrick just wanted to put new girls with more experienced partners, that's all."

Pam reacted hotly. "*I've* got lots of experience dancing with guys—"

Leah couldn't resist a long, pointed look at Pam's nails. Today they were trimmed short, though still painted a shrill red. Pam caught Leah's eyes on her hands and quickly hid them behind

her back, then met her stare with a defiant gaze
of her own.

"That's why I'm not interested in dancing with
a creep like James. He dropped me on purpose
the other day," she fumed and reddened at the
memory. "He's so self-centered he could be bad
for a girl's health! Even if he is Romeo!"

Leah started to point out that Pam's nails and
not James's manners were the reason he dumped
her on the floor during class, but Katrina inter-
vened. The slight, pale-cheeked dancer was an-
gling with the other girls to get a better view of
her hair in the mirror. She stopped braiding her
hair and turned around. "Pam, no one knows
James is going to be Romeo. I think you're jumping to some pretty drastic conclusions. At the
moment all I care about is going out there and
dancing my best. After all, Juliet isn't the only
student part in the demonstration," she said sen-
sibly. "And I don't think anyone's been stealing
anyone else's partner, either."

Leah's whole body tensed as she waited for
Pam's reaction. Pam just stood there gaping at
Katrina, obviously surprised that the soft-spoken
girl dared contradict her.

Katrina looped each of her braids into a doughnut shape above her ears and fastened them tightly
with hairpins. "Patrick assigned Leah to James
because they work well together," she continued.
"James is going into the company next year. He
probably wants him to get more experience."

Before Pamela or Leah could say another word,
Linda picked up where Katrina left off. "And none
of us need all this commotion before a tryout."

All the other girls except Pamela agreed.

Pamela rolled her eyes and let out a loud disgusted sigh. Then she beckoned imperiously to Mindy and Abigail, and the three of them swept past the others, out of the room into the studio.

After they left no one said a word.

Leah looked at the clock above the mirror and panicked. Just three more minutes. First Alex, then Katrina, Linda, and Mary Ellen filed out to begin their warm-ups. Leah hurried to put on her tights, feeling a little embarrassed at her outburst. What was getting into her anyway? One month at SFBA and all her resolve to follow Hannah Greene's advice and not get embroiled in petty, jealous conflicts had been forgotten. Leah hastily put up her hair, jabbing bobby pins into her scalp in her rush to get ready on time. She was the last one out of the dressing room when the call for the audition finally came.

Chapter 4

Leah was never sure how it hap-
pened. One minute she was flying through the
air in an exhilarating combination of brisés and
assemblés. The next minute she was flat on her
back on the floor, too stunned to move or to
think.

She heard Linda gasp from somewhere behind
her, then saw the black girl's feet dance by just
before she closed her eyes. Somewhere in the
back of her mind she remembered that if you fall
at an audition, you're supposed to get up and
pretend that nothing happened. Her friend Kay
had actually fallen in front of Madame Preston
during the entrance auditions. Kay's poise and
quick recovery helped win her entry into the
school. Leah remembered that and still didn't
move. Finally, as if from a great distance, she
heard Patrick's sharp command to Robert, the
accompanist. The next second the music stopped.

Then Patrick's strong hand was on hers and as she opened her eyes, his friendly brown eyes were looking down at her, filled with concern. "Leah?" he asked. "Can't you get up?" Leah was aware that Robert was beside him, along with Diana Chen, the other teacher and judge, and Alexandra. Some part of Leah registered that everyone except Diana looked really worried. Diana looked annoyed.

For a moment Leah couldn't find the voice to answer. She sat up slightly, leaning on her elbows. Patrick let out a long, relieved sigh, but Leah still couldn't respond to him. Everything hurt, though even before she wiggled her toes and worked her ankles around in a circle—first her right, then her left—she knew she was a little bruised, shaken, but not really injured. Slowly the realization dawned on her: she had just flubbed her audition. She looked up at Patrick quickly, a frown creasing her high forehead. "I'm sorry," she murmured, feeling hot all over and more humiliated than she'd felt in her entire life. The next moment an incredible sense of relief washed over her. *I don't have to worry about James anymore, or Pam, or Alex, or anyone. I can't possibly be Juliet now.* She repeated the words a couple of times to herself and felt her whole body relax. Then she caught Pamela Hunter's eye. She was standing outside the circle of girls with her hands planted on her hips. She was actually *smirking* at Leah. Looking at Pam, Leah got a crazy thought. *Pam made me slip.* The idiotic accusation rattled around in her aching head for a moment, then

Leah dismissed it. Pam hadn't *done* a thing. She couldn't have. Pam had been four dancers in front of Leah. Still, there was no doubt that Pam was very happy Leah had just blown her chances at getting a role in the dance demonstration program.

Something inside Leah snapped into focus. She sat up straight and brusquely rubbed her elbows, which stung like crazy. She would show Pam, and the rest of the world, that one fall wasn't going to get her down. No way.

Leah balled her hand up into a fist and took a deep breath. Though her legs felt shaky, she scrambled to her feet, scorning Robert's proffered hand. "I'm okay," she said tightly. She dusted off her tights and shrugged her shoulders to loosen her back. "I'm okay."

"We don't need any heroics around here," Diana warned Leah. "Don't try to pretend you're okay if you're not. Dancing on an injury is just courting disaster." What Diana said made sense, but for some reason it made Leah determined to keep dancing even if her leg were broken. She had a feeling Diana would like to see her drop out now. Leah took a deep relaxing breath and made herself smile. Diana, a principal with the Bay Area Ballet company, was the one teacher at SFBA Leah had trouble with. Leah couldn't quite put her finger on Diana's subtly negative attitude toward her but figured it had something to do with Pam. Diana was one of the few teachers in the school who adored Pam.

"You can come back later this afternoon and audition with another group," Patrick suggested in a gentle voice. He kept his eye on Leah as she walked around trying to work out the kinks in her legs and back. "Yes," he continued after a moment's deliberation. "I think that would be best for you."

Leah whirled around and declared shrilly, "No. I just slipped. I'm okay. I really am." She stood as tall as she could and tried to project a healthy, undamaged image. Her head was beginning to pound, but the more it pounded, the braver she tried to look. "I'll go on. I'm ready now," she said, not really feeling ready but deciding she'd die before she'd let Pamela, or anyone else, catch on.

Diana looked at Leah as if she were crazy, then shrugged. "She slipped here," she said, pointing to the exact spot on the floor. Alex hurried over and ran her shoe lightly over the area.

"Like ice," was her verdict.

Katrina and Patrick brought some rosin and Alex worked the gritty substance around the slick patch on the floor with her shoe.

"Well, then—" Diana looked around and favored Pam with a smile. "If you're ready, let's get back to work. We'll take that last combination from the top: brisé, assemblé, two times, pose into an arabesque, fall, and begin again to the other side."

Diana raised her hand. Robert began the music. Somehow Leah muddled through. She wasn't dancing her best, but at least she was dancing. But as hard as she tried to regain her concentration, her fall had unnerved her and the audition went from bad to worse. Every time a combination ended to the right, Leah found herself facing left. She even fell off pointe once in the middle of a double pirouette. With every step she fought back the urge to give in and call it quits. She kept dancing mainly because she could feel Pam's eyes on her, gloating.

When it was over, Leah mechanically joined the other girls applauding Patrick and Diana, but she kept her eyes focused on the floor.

"Don't worry. Everyone has off days," Alex said softly as the applause died down.

Leah shook her head. "Not during an audition. I should have quit while I was ahead." She looked up at the tall Russian girl. Alex looked all blurry through her tears. "Besides"—a thought formed in Leah's head as she spoke— "I think I wanted to do badly. I was scared that I'd get picked, that everyone would hate me, that you wouldn't get the part even though you deserve it. I didn't want Pam to be able to say I told you so when the cast list was posted." Leah squeezed her hands together and forced back her tears. "I should have listened to you. I shouldn't have tangled with Pam in the dressing room. I lost my concentration. Now I've really blown it." Leah's voice wobbled and she averted her eyes from Alex. "If I were a judge, I wouldn't even cast me in one of the minor parts!" Leah cried.

"Nonsense," Alex declared firmly. "You're just upset. It's not your fault the floor was slippery." She waited to see if her words had any effect on the despondent Leah. "Leah," she continued with a sigh. "Count your blessings. You didn't get hurt.

An injury would be something to worry about." Almost to herself she added, "The powers that be around here aren't exactly thrilled when their prize dancers get sidelined."

Leah barely took in Alex's remarks. She was staring dully at the floor, grinding a tiny chip of rosin into dust with the toe of her pointe shoe.

Alex put her hand on Leah's shoulder and made her look up. "You can't let things like this get to you. You'll never survive here," Alex whispered in an urgent voice. "Do you understand?"

Leah didn't understand any of it—Pam's hostility, this imagined battle over James, Alex's talk about injuries—but she was too tired to discuss it. Her head was hurting more by the minute. She needed some aspirin fast. She tugged down the back of her leotard and opened the door to the dressing room.

The next group of auditionees pushed out past her. Some of the girls cast curious glances at Leah. She pursed her lips and pretended not to notice, but her cheeks reddened with shame. Thanks to Pam, the whole school was going to find out how the "Great Stephenson," as Pam called her mockingly, had fallen flat on her back performing an elementary combination.

Chapter 5

"Here she is at last!" Pamela Hunter cried the next morning. Her voice carried easily above the general din in the school's front hall. "Of course the 'Great Stephenson' really didn't need to be in a rush to find out the big news. Congratulations, Leah, or should I say 'Juliet'?" Pam oozed. She plunged through the knot of dancers toward Leah, her hand extended like a claw.

Leah's mouth fell open. "Juliet?" Her heart quickened. She had walked to school by the most roundabout route, trying to put off looking at the call-board. She was sure her name wouldn't be on it. She had psyched herself up for defeat. But now Pam was congratulating her.

Ignoring Pam's hand, Leah pushed past the southern girl and proceeded toward the bulletin board. It was empty this morning except for an official-looking typed list pinned dead center. As

she neared it, the little crowd of girls parted.
Their faces were generally friendly, if envious.

"Good show!" Linda grinned.

Katrina gave her a warm hug.

"I told you so!" Melanie Carlucci, Kay's room-
mate, said in a singsong voice, and gave Leah's
shoulder an affectionate slap.

Abigail and Mindy just glared at her.

One look at the list explained why. Neither girl
had gotten any part in the first cast. Then Leah
smiled. Alex and Kay had. The were both slated,
with Linda and another girl Leah knew just by
sight, to take part in the ballet class demonstration, as what Kay fondly dubbed the "Barre Belles."
Leah ran her finger down the list. The smile on
her face broadened when she actually saw her
name in capital letters, centered on the page:

LEAH STEPHENSON—JULIET in pas de deux from
Romeo and Juliet

Pam hadn't been putting her on. She had gotten
the part. At the moment she had no idea why, but
she wasn't going to let herself care. Alex had
been right after all. Flubbing the audition wasn't
the end of the world. Her dancing in general was
good enough to merit some reward.

Her eye traveled farther down the page, looking
for James's name. No boys were listed, but no
wonder Pam was in such a good mood. Just below Leah's name Pam's appeared. She had secured the other big role. She would dance the
tricky mazurka with the big jumps from *Les*

Sylphides that all the girls had just learned in repertoire class. Pam was the only new student who had mastered it so far.

"Of course *I* got the big solo!" Pam said smugly. Leah counted to ten before turning around. The reason Pam had deigned to congratulate her was suddenly apparent: dancing with someone else didn't count quite as much in Pam's book as hogging the whole stage to herself. Leah was about to blow up, when she remember again Miss Greene's advice not to become involved in petty arguments and rivalries. Leah had already blown an audition by getting worked up over Pam. She wasn't about to let anything like that happen again.

"Congratulations, Pam," she said sweetly. "You do dance the mazurka beautifully."

Pam soaked up the compliment like a sponge and smiled a languorous smile. But her green eyes were narrowed to two slits. "Thank you," she drawled, adjusting the collar of her brilliant blue silk blouse. "And to think little old me got that part without friends in high places." She fastened her eyes on Leah and kept smiling. "It's so—so satisfying!"

Leah's resolve not to argue with Pam evaporated. "I was chosen for Juliet, Pam, because I'm suited for it," Leah defended herself hotly. "I know I blew that audition yesterday, but one bad performance doesn't mean you're not made of the right stuff to be a dancer."

Pam put up her hands and backed off, looking

apologetic and innocent. Leah balled up her fist in the pockets of her sweatshirt and tried to keep her temper as Pam said, "Did I say that?" Pam looked around at the other girls. Most of them avoided her glance. "Stephenson, you're so thin-skinned. I never said you were a bad dancer. It's just that you *do* have James on your side. Around here that matters." Pam reached over and tapped the casting list with her finger. "This proves it! It isn't like *I* wanted the part."

Leah raised her eyes to the ceiling at Pam's lie. "Come off it, Pam," she cried in disgust.

Pam pretended not to hear. "Katrina, or Abigail, or Alex could have danced it as well as you." Pam's voice abruptly stopped and she looked over Leah's shoulder. "Speak of the devil. Alex, where have you been? Have you seen the casting list yet?"

Leah spun around. Alex was at the foot of the stairs. *Where had she been?* Leah wondered. Alex hadn't congratulated her. Then she noticed Alex's face. It was pale and drawn and her hands were wrapped so tightly around the handle of her bag, her knuckles were white. Leah's breath stopped a moment. Then Alex flashed her a thin smile.

Pam kept talking. She was saying something about Leah buttering up James, trying to get him in her corner, to fight her fights for her. But Leah wasn't paying any attention. Her eyes were fixed on Alex, and she was trying to figure out what to say or do. Leah had never seen Alex look so hurt and defeated. All at once Leah remembered their

conversation on the lawn a couple of days ago.
Alex had wanted to dance Juliet more than anything in the world. She must feel incredibly hurt
that Leah had gotten the part and she hadn't, and
after all of her brave, offhand remarks that Leah's
fall during the audition didn't mean a thing. Deep
down inside she must have been hoping that she
herself would get the role. Leah felt terrible. But
what could she do about it? Suddenly Pam's dumb
accusations weren't important to Leah anymore.
Alex was Leah's friend, and Leah had a terrible
feeling that if she didn't go up to Alex and say
something soon, their friendship might actually
end.

Before Leah could make her way to Alex, a
familiar, delighted shriek filled the hall. *"Leah!"*
Kay cried from over by the pay phone. "There
you are!" She slammed down the receiver. "I was
just calling the boardinghouse to see where you
were." She ran over and whacked Leah's back
with a congratulatory thump. "You got it! You got
it! I knew you would. And I got a part, too, and so
did Alex!" Kay grabbed Leah's hands and spun
her around in a circle. The few girls left in the
hall began to laugh. Kay suddenly looked embarrassed. She pulled Leah over to the corner. "Can
you believe it? We're going to have so much fun,
you, me, Alex—" She lowered her voice to a
hoarse whisper. "Of course, wouldn't you know
Pam will be dancing with us all, too." She wrinkled her turned-up nose and shrugged. "We'll have
fun in spite of her." Kay regarded Leah and looked
puzzled. "Hey, you don't look very happy."

Leah gave Kay's hand a grateful squeeze. "Listen, Kay, I'm happy." She tried to sound as if she meant it. "But we'll talk about all the fun we'll have later. Madame's class starts soon. I've—I've got to talk to Alex."

The tall Russian girl's back was disappearing behind the staircase. Leah didn't have time to explain anything to Kay. She dashed after Alex, and caught up with her, going up the seldom-used back stairs that led off the small cafeteria to the studios above.

"Alex!" Leah cried from the bottom step. On the narrow landing where the stairs turned, Alex stopped. Leah watched her shoulders heave as she took a deep breath. When she turned around, her face looked fairly calm, but her eye makeup had streaked her right cheek. Alex had been crying. Leah was shocked and for a moment she couldn't say a thing. She suddenly felt so guilty, as if she had stolen something of value from her best friend. Her first impulse was to apologize. A moment later she felt a little crazy.

"Alex, this is nuts. I feel like apologizing for getting that role...." Her voice trailed off. She stood there zipping and unzipping her sweatshirt, feeling like a fool. She couldn't be anything but honest with Alex.

Alex brushed her comment aside with a wave of her hand. She hooked her fingers in the belt loops of her slim black jeans and sighed. "Don't apologize, Leah. Only one person could dance Juliet out of the first cast." Alex paused and studied her narrow black ankle boots. She looked up and managed a smile. "Congratulations on getting it. You deserve the part no matter what anyone thinks." With that Alex started up the stairs again.

"Alex." Leah scrambled up a few steps and craned her neck around the corner of the landing. "I want to talk to you. Please don't be angry with me."

"I'm not angry," Alex said without turning around. She doubled her speed up the stairs, taking them two at a time. Leah watched her disappear and her heart sank.

"Yes, you are," she whispered. She sat down on the steps and burst into tears.

Kay found her a few minutes later. "What's wrong?" The diminutive girl hurried up the steps and plopped down by Leah's side. Leah couldn't answer. Her thin shoulders shook with her sobs. Kay sat very still beside her and waited for her tears to subside. Finally Leah looked up and gratefully accepted the tissue Kay handed her.

"Hey," Kay ventured in a teasing voice, "I think you're taking this tragedy of *Romeo and Juliet* too seriously!"

Leah couldn't even smile. She stared at her hands and pulled at the tissue until it tore. Soon she was shredding it in tiny bits. Fascinated, she watched them flutter to the step below. "Class is going to start soon," she said in a dead voice. She made no effort to move.

"I know that," Kay responded calmly. "So why don't we talk about what's wrong now."

Leah took a deep breath and began. She told Kay about Alexandra and how supportive she had been the past couple of days about Leah's chances for getting the part. "Now that I got it, she's mad at me. And it hurts." Leah's voice began to tremble.

Kay put her hand on Leah's shoulder and gently turned her around to face her. Kay's dark blue eyes searched Leah's, and she smiled. "Leah, of course Alex is upset. Everyone is. Not because *you* got the part, but because they didn't."

"Tell Pam Hunter that one!" Leah laughed bitterly.

Kay groaned. "Okay. We'll leave Pam and her sidekicks out of this discussion. As far as I'm concerned, she's not worth talking about anyway."

"But it's not Pam you're crying about?" Kay posed the question.

Leah shook her head. "No," she admitted sadly. "No way."

Kay leaned her elbows back on the step above her and pondered a moment before going on. "I guess it's all right to tell you this," she began slowly. "Last night I was talking to Melanie, and she told me that Alex has had the lead in these school demonstrations for the past two years."

Leah looked up sharply. "She never mentioned that."

"I know. And last year she danced with James. They actually did a pas de deux from *Swan Lake*." Kay sounded impressed.

Leah closed her eyes. "That must have been beautiful," she said aloud, picturing her dark-haired friend in a snow-white tutu partnered by a dark, velvety-looking James. Alex was born to dance *Swan Lake*.

"Melanie said they stole the show. Even the two company members—I think it was Carmen Martinez and Lou Evans—didn't get half as much applause for whatever they danced."

"No wonder she's so upset. First she loses James as a partner, and now—" Leah broke off.

"And now she won't get to dance Juliet. She had her heart set on it and it hurts," Kay said simply. "But she'll get over it. Just give her a little time."

Leah shook her head. "I don't know about that. I don't know that I would get over it so fast."

Kay dismissed Leah's fears with a laugh. She stood up and shook out the full corduroy skirt she was wearing and tucked in her blouse. "Don't be ridiculous. You'd get over it. So would I. Pam wouldn't—but then, we aren't going to talk about Pam." Kay shoved up her cuff and looked at her watch. Her round eyes got even bigger. "We are really going to be crying if we don't get upstairs fast and into class."

Leah stood up slowly. For the first time since she'd arrived at the school she felt like skipping class. Kay started up the stairs and reached her hand back for Leah's. "Come on, you can't mope about this all day. You should be happy."

Leah gave Kay a withering look.

Kay giggled. "Really." Her face turned serious as she said, "Don't worry about Alexandra. Let her nurse her wounds awhile, then talk to her. Have a good heart-to-heart. Be up front. I think she'd like that."

"If you say so." Leah was skeptical but she knew Kay was right. Talking to Alex after the dust settled was the only thing she could do.

"And by the way," Kay prattled on merrily, "I've got some incredible news."

Leah couldn't help but smile. The world could be ending but Kay's scoop of the day would somehow hog the headlines around the school.

"I found out about the boys."

"The boys?" Leah repeated.

Kay bobbed her head enthusiastically. "James is Romeo, of course."

Leah swallowed hard. "Of course."

"But the rest is positively unfair."

"Why?"

"Did you know they didn't even have auditions?" Kay asked as they hurried up the last few steps into the back hall.

"That is unfair," Leah commented.

"Well, every last one of them is going to be in the program."

Leah was truly surprised. "Are you kidding?"

Kay shook her head. "The demonstration class will be four girls and six boys. Four other boys will dance something Patrick has choreographed for them before Pam goes on. And then there's James."

"But that doesn't give a proper picture of ballet." Leah looked perplexed. "There aren't twice as many boys as girls here."

"I know," Kay moaned. "But they want to give these high school boys out there in the 'real' world the idea that ballet can be manly and appropriate for them, too."

Leah rolled her eyes, but before she could say anything else, she spied Robert entering the Blue Studio. "We're late!" she and Kay gasped in unison and tore down the hall, pulling their clothes off and stripping down to their dance clothes before even getting into the dressing room.

Chapter 6

On the stroke of four that afternoon Leah walked into the small third-floor rehearsal studio and knew immediately her day was about to go from bad to worse. As if it hadn't been bad enough to have Alex ignore her after morning class, she got her geometry quiz back from Mr. Creighton with an unnecessarily large C-minus scrawled in red over the top. Now Diana, not Patrick, seemed to be in charge of Leah's first rehearsal with James. The prospect of being coached by the one teacher who didn't seem to like her didn't appeal to Leah at all. The porcelain-skinned dancer's dark head was bent over Robert's at the piano. As she spoke to the pianist, she beat a sharp staccato rhythm on the score with a pencil. She didn't seem to notice Leah was there.

Leah dumped her bag in the corner and stood still a moment, not quite sure what to do. She had never been at a rehearsal with just another dancer, a coach, and an accompanist before. James was already in the room, warming up at the barre. Though he was facing Leah when she walked in, he continued to stare at the wall, his chin slightly tilted up. He didn't bother to acknowledge her presence. Leah clenched her fists and shook her head. The other girls might envy her dancing with James, but they certainly couldn't envy her having to put up with him. He was so utterly impolite. Working for the next few months with someone who didn't even have the courtesy to say hello was going to be just wonderful, Leah thought ruefully. Well, whatever James did or didn't do when they weren't actually *dancing* together was none of her business. She had enough to worry about right now. The first thing she needed to do was warm up. She could learn that much from James, she told herself. If she could become half as single-minded and directed as her partner, then working with him under such unpleasant circumstances would be worth it. She took a deep breath and straightened her shoulders. She smoothed back her hair with a tight gesture of annoyance and marched across the floor to the barre on the opposite side of the room from James, as far away from him as she could get.

A few minutes later Diana clapped her hands. She smiled a thin welcoming smile at Leah, but her face brightened like the sun as she greeted James. She beckoned them toward the center of the room, where she sat straddling a metal chair. Leah instantly noted the difference between the atmosphere in the little studio and in class: it was

looser, more relaxed. James was actually wearing
nonregulation dance gear: gray sweat pants over
his tights; a frayed red thermal shirt with cut-off
sleeves instead of the usual plain white T-shirt,
and a white terry sweat band. In Madame Preston's classes headbands for guys and girls were
taboo. Diana didn't seem to care. Leah felt very
awkward and like the student she was in her
plain pink tights, tank-top black leotard and pink
toe shoes. Out of habit she had peeled off her leg
warmers halfway through warm-up.

"Welcome, both of you," Diana said, pinning
her silky hair up in a chignon. "We have less than
a week to prepare this program. In fact, the first
performance will be next Tuesday afternoon."

Leah barely suppressed a gasp. "So soon?" she
squeaked, her hand flying to her throat with the
shock of it. She had been working with partners
only a month now, and with James only a couple
of days. She had danced in public as a soloist or
with a corps of girls only at Hannah Greene's
recitals. Tuesday seemed just a few hours away.

Diana gave her a pitying look. "Don't blame
me." She shrugged. "That's how these demos always go. Every year we do them, each year we
treat them like a last-minute surprise. We always
get about a week to prepare them. That's why we
select variations that you students are already
working on in class. Patrick tells me you've both
got a good general idea of the *Romeo and Juliet*
pas de deux, and really just need more practice
and polish." Diana breathed out a sigh and glanced
at the clock. "A week of rehearsal won't polish it

enough, but that's good, too. When you work as professional dancers you won't have much time for things. I've heard of ballerinas who have had to dance their first full-length *Swan Lake* on less then ten days' coaching."

"Are you serious?" Leah exclaimed, horrified at the thought. James let out an affected snort. Leah suddenly felt very naive.

Diana regarded her with a tolerant smile. "Dead serious, my dear. So you two had better be prepared to put in a lot of practice time of your own between now and next week. I brought my cassette player so you can record Robert's music." She stood up and stretched, then dragged the chair over to the piano. Leah noticed James didn't offer to help. She suddenly felt a bit smug: at least she wasn't the only person in the world he wasn't polite to. "First let me see you dance the whole thing once through. I want to get a picture of exactly how much work you need and how much help from me. Don't worry if you make mistakes. Just keep dancing."

She looked directly at Leah as she said that, and Leah felt her cheeks grow hot. She kept her eyes down and took her position stage right in the room. She tried to clear her mind and just think of the choreography as Robert began to play. Leah counted three measures and raised her head and downstage arm slowly in a yearning gesture. Diagonally across the room, James was smiling at her—a warm, enticing smile. Leah smiled back.

She took the first halting steps of the dance as

Juliet, unsure who was lurking in the shadows. Recognizing her Romeo, she flew across the room into his arms. His strong hands circled her waist and the first lift felt effortless, as if they were dancing with one body. Dancing with James there could be no slip-ups, no mistakes. Every step, every gesture, felt sure and natural. When the music ended, Leah's heart was pounding. They held their ending pose for what seemed like forever, and the room was silent except for the chirp of birds outside the open gabled window. The magic lingered until Diana cleared her throat. Then James gave a quick shake of his head and dropped Leah's hand. Rubbing the back of his smooth neck, he strutted off to the barre and grabbed a towel.

Leah blinked at the abrupt transition: Romeo to James. Would she ever get used to it?

She was still breathing hard and wiped the sweat off her brow with the back of her hand. Smoothing stray wisps of hair off her temples, she looked toward Diana for criticism. The expression on the older dancer's face made Leah's blood run cold. Inadvertently Leah took a couple of small steps backward and held her breath. Diana looked so angry. *Oh no!* Leah thought, *What have I done?* Frantically her mind ran over every phrase she had just danced. It had felt so right, but the pas de deux had gone by in a kind of blur—like everything did once she had learned the steps and danced them full out with James. She must have made a lot a mistakes. She had been so swept up in her dance with her partner, she had lost sight of what she was supposed to be doing. Leah let out her breath and braved another glance up at Diana.

Diana's face was passive now, as if the anger Leah had witnessed a moment before had never existed.

"Not bad!" James remarked to Diana. He graced Leah with a superior smile, then bowed his head slightly in her direction and said, "We haven't practiced our bows yet. That's very important." He sounded very businesslike and serious.

Leah eyed him with suspicion. Was he serious? How could he talk about bows when whatever they had danced just now was bad enough to provoke such strong reaction from Diana.

Diana obviously agreed with Leah, on this score at least. "Bows, Mr. Cummings," she said with exaggerated politeness," come *after* you have danced well enough to earn them." She then launched into a list of things that had gone wrong. Leah cringed with every word. Though she mentioned one or two points James could improve on, her comments made it quite clear that Leah was the person who had a lot of work to do to make this pas de deux presentable. Making it good was obviously out of the question.

Leah fought back the tears welling up in her eyes. When Diana finished, Leah glanced over at James, afraid to see his reaction to the coach's critique. She was surprised to see him looking at her as if he felt sorry for her. Leah started back to her corner, assuming they were going to begin the pas de deux again.

Diana marched across the room, pushing Leah not very gently out of her way. "Watch me!" she ordered. She clapped her hands together sharply. "Robert! James!" Then she took the opening position of the dance.

The music began and Leah watched Diana carefully as she ran through the number from beginning to end. Leah had half-expected the ballerina to mark the steps. As far as Leah knew, she wasn't even warmed up. But she danced full-out, throwing herself at James with great force and abandon. James looked as surprised as Leah, and twice his sure hands slipped. He nearly dropped Diana from the closing overhead lift.

"Sorry," he muttered the moment the music stopped. Diana glared at him. Her shoulders lifted as she took a deep annoyed breath. Then she whirled around and faced Leah. "Do you see how to do it now?" Diana watched the puzzlement on Leah's face deepen. She laughed. "Your port de bras, my dear, was all wrong," she remarked in a condescending voice.

Leah squinted at Diana. "My port de bras?" she repeated, not quite sure she'd heard right. Only the other day Madame Preston had said her arms were like Markova's. "You danced that whole piece full-out because my port de bras was wrong?" Leah gaped at the instructor. "I don't even know what parts I did wrong." The hard look on Diana's face stopped Leah from saying more.

James shocked her next by coming to her defense. "She's right, Diana," he said in his deep voice. "You shouldn't have made me dance the whole thing again because of some little problem with Leah's arms. I thought she had the choreography Patrick taught just right."

"What you think doesn't count just now, James," Diana retorted angrily. "In case you have forgotten, you're not a member of the company yet. You're still a student in this school and I'm a teacher."

James suddenly looked scared, as if something in Diana's words contained a veiled threat. He backed off and said, "I'm sure you've got your reasons." He looked from Leah to Diana and back to Leah again and the little crease between his eyebrows deepened. He went to the barre and bent over to stretch out his back.

Diana ordered Leah to the corner and asked her to mark out the steps again with James. Leah obeyed without question. Years of dance training had disciplined her enough for that, though inside she began to seethe. Leah knew she hadn't danced the pas de deux perfectly. She knew there was plenty of room for improvement. But her arms? Why did Diana keep harping on the one strong point Leah knew she had?

Until the last run-through of the afternoon's rehearsal Diana didn't let her dance full-out with James once. Two more times Diana elbowed Leah aside, insisting on showing her the correct interpretation of the steps and music. With only moments left of their allotted rehearsal time, James finally spoke up.

"Diana, I'm dancing this program with *Leah* next week, not you." There was a cutting edge to this voice that visibly took Diana off guard. "So I think for this last go-around, I'd better dance it full-out with her." He imperiously motioned Leah to the corner and nodded to Robert.

The accompanist looked doubtful and glanced at Diana. Her expression was impassive but her walk was tight and angry as she marched back to the piano. She hoisted herself up on the edge of the baby grand and with a curt wave of her hand commanded Robert to begin.

Afterward, James didn't let go of her hand, even when Robert got up and folded his music. Diana stayed in the front of the room, obviously expecting something. James ignored her. He looked down at Leah and said in a clear, haughty voice, "That was perfect, just perfect."

Diana cleared her throat and Leah remembered they were supposed to clap. Applauding the teacher was always proper protocol after class, so she figured it must be after rehearsals, too. She brought her hands together without much enthusiasm. Before they finished, Diana swept into the dressing room. Leah lingered behind, reluctant to spend time with Diana alone. She also wanted to see if James would stay friendly.

He didn't. He grabbed his things and headed into the hall without even saying good-bye.

Leah knew she couldn't stay in the studio forever. Dancers from the company had scheduled rehearsal time in the coveted space. She squared her shoulders and mustered up her courage to enter the changing room a few doors down the hall.

Though Diana had been tough, and though Leah wished she had gotten more time to actually dance with James, she had picked up pointers from watching the ballerina dance the role that had been created for her by the company's resident choreographer the spring before. Unlike some of the other girls, Leah hadn't seen it danced by anyone but students until now, and Diana's phrasing had been beautiful. It was different from what Leah had imagined. After watching Diana, her own movements had become more expansive and broad and she actually felt more passionate during the last run-through with James.

Diana didn't look around when Leah opened the door. The Asian girl was already dressed and was busy brushing her long straight hair in front of the mirror.

Quiet as a mouse Leah went to her chair and began changing her clothes.

Diana looked at Leah in the mirror and spoke without facing her. "Not bad for a first rehearsal."

Leah was shocked. "Uh—thank you," she murmured, wondering why Diana had acted as if nothing had gone right all afternoon. Was that just her way of pulling the best out of her students, Leah wondered as she poked her head through the neck of her baggy blue sweater.

"Of course, you're not quite as suited to the choreography as some dancers," Diana said almost kindly.

"I feel so natural dancing those steps," Leah countered with a frown.

Diana shrugged and said, "It was all choreographed on me, you know, and you and I aren't alike at all."

Leah could only agree with that. Except—and she carefully scrutinized Diana's slim body—they were the exact same size and build. In fact, after class today Leah had made a quick trip up to Mrs. Howard, the company's wardrobe mistress, to be measured for Juliet's filmy gown. Mrs. Howard had told her she could wear Diana's costume and it wouldn't even have to be tailored. When she tried it on, it fit like a glove and felt as if it had been made for her. Just like the steps to the ballet.

Keeping her eye on Leah in the mirror, Diana said very slowly, "Pam's more the kind of dancer I could see in that part."

Leah let out an involuntary groan, then buried her head quickly in her dance bag, pretending to look for her hair brush. Diana was crazy. Among the top students in Madame Preston's class, Pam was least suited to the lyrical choreography. She was a strong, hard, athletic dancer. Juliet's choreography was quiet, subtle, requiring soft arabesques, beautiful lines, and exquisite balances, —all of Pam's weakest points. When Leah felt she had regained control of herself, she looked up. "You were one of the judges," she said with amazing sweetness. "How come you didn't pick her?"

Diana scowled. "It wasn't totally up to me. The votes were two to one—Patrick *and* James." She cut herself off and glared at Leah. "Just because some people here believe you are the most talented person to walk the earth since"—Diana searched for the most ludicrous comparison she could come up with—"Since Pavlova, it doesn't mean you are. That attitude will get you nowhere. Half the dancers in this school are as good as you are. Pam has a much better jump than you and more passion in her dancing."

Two little red spots blossomed on Leah's cheeks. Pamela Hunter wasn't a better dancer. Leah was sure of that! Diana didn't give her a chance to defend herself, she just barreled on. "Not that I'm saying you don't have talent," she added, finally satisfied that her hair was hanging just right. "But other girls, like Pam, or Alex, or even Katrina could have made as much of this role as you. Don't forget that."

Leah didn't know how to respond. She felt angry and humiliated. At the same time, she couldn't help but hear some truth in Diana's brutal outburst.

"I know that, Diana," Leah said, managing to sound very calm.

"Good," Diana said. "And work on those arms. You just might make something of yourself yet."

With that the young ballerina walked out of the room and slammed the door so hard the partition shuddered. Leah listened until the sound of her footsteps faded away down the hall. Then the tears that had been building up for over an hour began to flow down her cheeks. She wiped them away but more came. She cried silently the whole time she finished dressing. Why was everything about this dance demonstration going so wrong? First Pam this morning, then Alex, now Diana acting as if she had no right even to attempt the part. All afternoon Leah couldn't figure out if Diana had been trying to help or hurt her. James at least had said the rehearsal had gone well. He had said that in spite of Diana's petulant mood. Leah walked up to the mirror and freshened her makeup, dabbing the spots near her eyes where her mascara had run.

When she opened the dressing room door, James was standing outside, leaning against the opposite wall, smiling at her.

"What are you doing here?" she asked, looking to the left, then the right, down the hall. No one else was in sight.

"Waiting for you."

Leah frowned and started for the stairs. James followed a few paces behind her. With one foot on the top step she turned around and asked over her shoulder. "Why?"

"You must be tired. I know I am. Do you want a ride home?"

"*You* want to give *me* a ride home?" She laughed a bit shrilly.

"Did I miss the joke?" James asked archly, and continued just behind her down the stairs.

Leah didn't bother to turn around this time. "Listen, James, I like dancing with you. I think you like dancing with me."

"I do," he concurred with a hint of enthusiasm in his snobbish voice.

Leah barreled on. "But as soon as the music stops, you act as if I don't even exist." They had reached the bottom step. The only sign of life on the ground floor was the whistle of a teapot in the cafeteria and the tap of a typewriter in one of the back offices.

She whirled around quickly and found herself only inches away from James's muscular chest. She backed off a couple of steps and planted her hands on her hips. "So why this sudden change? What have I done to deserve such a favor?" She heard the words come out of her mouth all hard and sarcastic and felt bad about it. But not bad enough to apologize to James. Not after the day she'd had. She just wanted to get home and go to her room and be alone. James had had an apparent change of heart. But his timing definitely stank.

"We're going to work together," he said, oblivious to her sarcasm. "I thought we should get to know each other. Alex says you aren't half bad."

"Alex says *I'm* not half bad!" Leah cried, feeling betrayed by her friend. The idea that Alex talked to James about her was infuriating, even though she had said pretty much the same thing to Leah about James.

"And you aren't. I like you."

James started for the door. Leah remained rooted to the spot, dumbfounded—especially when James actually held it open for her. "I give up. I'm tired. I'll take you up on your offer," she said, giving her dance bag a tug and stalking past James.

He led her across the parking lot to a nondescript beige station wagon.

"Is this your car?" Leah blurted out, surprised. She had expected something with more snob appeal, like a Mercedes or an Alfa Romero. Something expensive, fast, and sleek.

James opened the door and replied, "My car's in the shop—as usual. I borrowed this heap from my landlady."

Leah nodded, not really interested. She had taken up his offer for a ride because she was tired, far too tired to argue about why she didn't feel like accepting a lift from him. They drove the short distance in silence, with Leah still fuming over Diana's harsh words.

When James pulled up in front of Mrs. Hanson's, Leah got out quick. "Thanks," she said curtly, and started down the walk.

James poked his head out of the passenger window and shouted after her. "What are you doing Saturday?"

"Dancing with you all morning, remember? Patrick booked us into the A studio."

James smiled enticingly and Leah cocked her head. "I didn't mean that, stupid," he said almost gently. "I meant afterward. There's an exhibition of Degas paintings and prints at the museum. Want to go?"

Leah's eyes grew huge with surprise. She was tired and depressed and not in the mood to think about Saturday, but she also was curious about James—the new James, the one who talked to her in the hall, drove her home, and now was acting almost human. Suddenly he seemed not so distantly related to Romeo she had danced with less than an hour ago. Saturday afternoon at the museum seemed like an interesting idea.

"Uh, sure. That would be nice," Leah accepted, suddenly feeling awkward.

"Great," James said, then swung the car around in a wide U-turn and vanished down the steep hill.

Leah looked after him a moment and blinked. Had she been dreaming? Had James actually asked her out? At the thought Leah started blushing. From inside the boardinghouse the peal of Mrs. Hanson's dinner bell rang out. "It's not really a *date*, Stephenson," she muttered, and hurried up the front steps not sure if that realization made her happy or sad.

Chapter 7

Leah paused for a moment on the second-floor landing of the boardinghouse. The setting sun filled the round stained-glass window at the end of the hall and tinted the creamy walls a lovely pink. But Leah didn't notice. She was staring at Alex's door, trying to work up the nerve to knock. The Russian girl hadn't shown up for dinner, though according to the sign-in sheet on the entrance hall table she had been home for hours. Leah had no way of knowing if enough time had passed since that morning for Alex to nurse her wounds. She knew her mother would tell her to let Alex sleep on it. But Leah was too impatient for that. She believed in getting difficult things over with fast, in clearing the air. She remembered once, when she was a little girl, her father had told her never to go to sleep angry. It hardened your heart, he had said. Her father had been dead for six years, but Leah cherished every word of advice he had given her.

She took a deep breath and with a determined set of her chin approached Alexandra's door.

Before she could tap on the door, it flew open and Alex started out. When she saw Leah standing there, her hand poised in the air, she let out a startled cry. Leah swallowed hard.

"Uh—hi." Leah spoke first and quickly looked down at her feet.

"Hi!" Alex responded, sounding equally embarrassed.

The two girls stood awkwardly in the doorway for a moment. Then they both began speaking at once.

"I was just coming to ..." they said almost in unison, then exchanged nervous smiles.

Leah looked into Alex's brightly decorated room. "Um, I think we should talk," she said before Alex could get out another word.

"Me, too." Alex shoved her hands in her jumpsuit pockets and beckoned Leah to follow her into the room.

Leah closed the door behind her and looked around. She always had a hard time reconciling Alex's taste in decor with Alex's taste in clothes. The tall, dark girl always dressed all in black or all in white, never anything else. Even the dramatically large dangling earrings she wore outside of class were either black or white, yet her room was a symphony of brilliant color. She had repapered her walls with contemporary paper patterned with bright geometric splashes of vivid yellow, fiery red, and electric blue. Her bedspread was the same blue, and her bed was heaped with cushions of magenta, shocking pink, purple, yellow, and green. The effect was initially jarring but strangely tasteful. Leah had decided more than once that should Alexandra decide not to be a ballerina, she'd become quite rich and famous as an interior decorator. Already she had displayed considerable talent with stage design, and had been chosen to do the sets for the following spring's student production of *Sleeping Beauty*. Leah knew for certain this version of the Tchaikovsky classic would definitely not be done in pastels.

Leah gingerly walked over to the nearest chair and sat down. She looked from the clock on the night table to Alex's neatly arranged desk, then over toward the oddly out-of-place old-fashioned rocking chair next to the window. Alex sat down on the edge of the bed. Finally Leah met her eyes. "I think we have some stuff to talk about," she said.

"We do." Alex's reply was almost eager. "We really do. But I wanted to say first that I'm sorry."

"Sorry?" Leah jumped to her feet and plopped down by Alex on the bed. "I'm the one who should be sorry. I got the part you really wanted and I didn't understand how much it meant to you to dance with James again this year, and to do this role. I didn't hear you really. Even though you told me. If only there were some way we both could have it!" Leah declared earnestly.

Alex groaned. "Leah, don't be a dope. We can't both have the role. We can't help but be in competition for some things. This time you got the prize—next time—" For a moment Alex's expressive eyes glinted with a challenge, then she glanced down at her hands and tried to look contrite. "Listen," she said, getting up off the bed. "I'm the one who should apologize. I wasn't very nice to you this morning."

Leah started to protest, but Alex silenced her with a look. "Hear me out," she ordered. "I couldn't help it. I felt hurt and disappointed. Not because *you* got the role, but because I didn't. It's hard to separate your feelings about these things." Alex folded her long arms across her chest and paced over to the window and back. She studied Leah, her strong chin set and her lips lightly pursed together. "You're the first real competition I've had since I got here," she said with a trace of her old arrogance. "It's hard when you're not the one who's Madame Preston's—or James Cummings's—favorite anymore."

Leah detected a faint note of bitterness in her friend's throaty voice that made her feel vaguely uncomfortable. Leah flashed on the picture of a younger girl coming to the school one or two years from now, a gifted dancer like herself, perhaps more talented, perhaps not. But new and fresh and the kind of person the SFBA staff would be very excited about. It was definitely an unsettling picture, and Leah put it out of her head as fast as she could.

Alex sat down again and went on in a more gentle voice. "This isn't easy to say, but you are absolutely the most perfect partner for James—and I'm not the only one who's noticed that," she added with a significant nod of her regal head.

Leah gaped at Alex a moment, then grinned with pleasure. "Thanks for the compliment." Her face grew serious. "I know you loved dancing with him, though."

Alex shrugged off Leah's concern. "That's true, but that's not my point. People will be jealous of you. The directors of the company have big plans for James. If they see you make a really great partner for him, well—" Alex started laughing at the expression on Leah's face. "Don't look so shocked. You know you have a brilliant future," Alex said, clasping her hands in a gesture typical of Madame Preston.

"What do you want, Alex. Buttering me up like this." Leah pretended to look suspicious.

Alex just laughed. She exaggerated her accent and said ominously. "You vill see." She flopped down on the bed and propped a couple of cushions under her head. Her voice grew thoughtful as she continued. "I'm not buttering you up. I'm warning you. Diana's jealous already."

Leah's mouth dropped open. "Jealous?" Even as she repeated the word she knew Alex was right, though why in the world the company's brightest young star should envy her at all was a mystery.

Alex walked her feet up the wall and stared

hard at the ceiling. "Yes. Very jealous. And that's not a good sign." She turned her head quickly toward Leah. "In case you haven't noticed, you and she are very similar types of dancers: you have the same strengths—great musicality, beautiful balance, clean, fast turns, good classic line."

"But Diana said—" Leah started to protest, then stopped herself. She got up from the bed and began fiddling with the stack of ribbons and barrettes on a tray on Alex's dresser. Diana had said a lot today: that Leah's port de bras wasn't good, that Leah and she weren't alike, that the choreography made specifically for her was all wrong for Leah's body type. None of Diana's comments made any sense at the time. But now they did. Jealousy. That explained a lot.

Leah had never dreamed that teachers and coaches and company members would be competitive with mere students like her. But now that Alex brought it up ...

Alex seemed to be reading her thoughts. "You're only about four years younger than she. That's quite a threat. What if you're in the company in two years or three? You'll be competing for all the same roles."

Leah didn't respond. She was trying to digest her friend's words. Part of her wanted to understand; part of her wanted desperately to change the subject. She frowned and twisted a button on one of the pockets of her painter's pants. She didn't like the direction this conversation was taking.

"I don't know anything about Diana," Leah said. "But I do know we're friends and I wanted to clear the air before we—" she stopped, and thought of her father's advice. "It's a bad thing to sleep on your anger," she concluded in a softer voice.

Alex visibly caught her breath. A remote, wistful look crossed her beautiful high-cheekboned face. A moment later it was gone. "My grandmother used to tell me that. It's an old Russian saying."

"An old American saying!" Leah countered playfully, then ducked the pillow Alex aimed in her direction.

"Well, I'm not angry anymore," Alex declared with an emphatic toss of her head.

"Me neither," Leah concurred with a relieved burst of laughter. "But you must be starved."

"I never starve!" Alex said, deepening her accent dramatically. "I am prepared!" She yanked open the cupboard in the wall beside her four-poster and pulled out a cookie tin and two bottles of Perrier. "They aren't cold," she said, pointing to the mineral water. "But it saves us a trip to the kitchen."

A moment later the two girls delved into Alex's private stash of granola bars and nut mix. After devouring her snack, Leah leaned back in the rocking chair and propped her feet next to Alex on the bed. "I'm glad we're friends again," she sighed happily.

"We have always been—and will always be —friends." Alex paraphrased Mr. Spock's famous words from *Star Trek* and toasted Leah with her half-emptied bottle of Perrier. "Live long," she said gravely, forming her fingers into the Vulcan salute, "and prosper!"

Leah chuckled, amazed as always at Alex's repertoire of trivia from American popular culture. Then she grew serious. She stared at the green bottle in her hands and sloshed the fizzy water around and around until it threatened to bubble out of the top. She took a sip and set the bottle down on the floor. "I don't know what I'd do around here without you to talk to," she said. She lifted her eyes toward Alex and grinned. "You're the old hand at this SFBA game. Sometimes I feel so hopelessly blind—and naive."

Alex crossed her legs under her on the bed and asked, "What's on your mind?"

"Pam."

Alex arched her eyebrows. "Her." Her tone left no doubt about exactly what she thought of the girl.

"Why does she always make so much trouble?"

Alex dismissed Leah's question with an expressive shrug. "Jealousy, I guess."

Leah made a face. "Ugh, that word again. Isn't anyone around here not jealous?" she asked in frustration.

"No."

Leah reluctantly accepted Alex's diagnosis. They shared a moment's companionable silence, then Leah spoke up. "No, it's not just that." She hooked her hands on the back of the chair and began rocking back and forth quickly. "Everyone around here is jealous of everyone else. But no one is as vicious as Pam. I'm not sure how I managed to do it, but I've made a real enemy out of her. I've never had an enemy before, and I don't know what to do about it. Any suggestions?"

Alex knelt straight up on the bed and looked around, a little wild-eyed. She lowered her voice to a conspiratorial whisper and motioned Leah closer. "Kill her!" she said in a exaggerated dramatic tone, then threw her head back and laughed heartily at the shocked expression of Leah's face.

"Sorry," she apologized as soon as she caught her breath. "I couldn't resist that," she confided with a delicious laugh. Then she folded her legs back under her, and bent over them, pillowing one side of her face on the bed. She grinned wickedly up at Leah.

Leah tried to look annoyed. "AAAl-ex," she moaned, drawing her friend's name out. "I'm serious."

Alex straightened up and folded her hands primly in her lap. "Okay, if it's serious you want to be ..." She smiled. "Then, Leah, you must let Pam roll off your back like a duck." As soon as the words were out of her mouth she frowned. Leah was shaking her head in disgust. "That's not right, is it?" Alex asked, sounding a little sheepish.

Leah let out an exaggerated sigh and said, "No. Like water off a duck's back."

Alex noted the correction, and Leah went on. "You keep saying that. All my friends, even Chrissy back home, tell me the same thing. Let her go.

Don't pay attention to her. But how can I do that when she's *soooooo* mean to me?" Leah tilted her head back and looked up at the ceiling. She continued through clenched teeth. "Pamela will stop at absolutely nothing to get to me. Today she tried to get between you and me. The other day she made me feel slimy and conniving just because I ended up dancing with James." Leah shuddered with distaste. "How can I just sit back and take it?"

"You don't have any choice. If you start acting like Pam, you'll turn into a horrible human being—and you can't afford that. It will ruin your dancing. And believe me, the way Pam acts will get her into trouble someday, too," Alex predicted.

Leah closed her eyes and expelled a long breath of defeat.

"You asked for my advice," Alex pointed out.

Leah didn't look very happy now that she heard it, but she admitted truthfully, "I didn't like it any better when Chrissy told me the same thing. But I guess you're both right."

Leah tucked her feet up under her and absently started unpinning her hair. Although she knew her friends were right, she had a feeling her relationship with Pam was something she would have to work out herself, in her own way, when the time was right.

A little while later Leah headed up to her room. On the top landing she remembered James. She turned around and almost rushed down again. She was dying to tell Alex that James had actually been nice to her and driven her home, and that

Saturday they planned to go to the museum together. But something stopped her. She wrinkled
her nose and suddenly felt embarrassed. For weeks
she had complained nonstop to Alex about snooty,
nasty James. Now she'd have to eat her words.
She was actually going out with him on a sort of
date. The prospect of confiding in Alex suddenly
wasn't very appealing. Besides, it would be much
more fun to see the shocked expression on Alex's
face when she came in Saturday night with James.

Chapter 8

"That went smoothly," Leah told James Saturday as they walked out of the Academy into the warm, breezy afternoon. Leah blinked a few times and shielded her eyes, wishing she had brought her sunglasses. She'd been inside so much the past few days rehearsing, her eyes hurt from the unaccustomed glare.

She let out a contented sigh. Their first solo rehearsal without Diana and Patrick had gone well. Actually *more* than well, Leah reflected. It had been perfect, exquisite, beautiful—and long. But Leah didn't mind. Today's intensive workout had further deepened her conviction that she was cut out, heart and soul, for the rigorous life of classical dance.

In some ways James had been even more demanding than Diana. He insisted on going over each phrase of the choreography at least ten times. By the end of the day Leah felt as if the pas de deux were as natural to her as walking. The sun was already low in the west, and the waters of the bay shone like a blanket of gold. Leah stopped at the edge of the walk to admire the view. She vaguely wondered if the museum was still open. She looked back at James to ask, and found him looking at her. He was smiling the same wonderful smile as when they danced together. Leah's heart suddenly felt light and airy. James should smile more often, she thought.

"You are the best partner I've ever danced with," James said, not taking his eyes off her. "And I've partnered girls already in the company. I wish you were going to be in the company next year." He hooked her hand through his arm and gave it a companionable squeeze.

Leah's heart raced with pride and satisfaction. Diana had been wrong. James's words strengthened Leah's own feeling. She knew she was right for the part of Juliet. She got the role not just because of James, and not in spite of Pam, but because she was the student best suited for the role. Leah could barely restrain herself from pirouetting exuberantly down the walk ahead of James.

The very next second Leah's heart stopped. Her rosy face whitened with dismay. No wonder Diana had been so tough on her the other day during rehearsal. When she saw Leah dance something real, something other than a classroom exercise, she went livid. Under her cool controlled exterior the Bay Area Ballet principal must have been in a rage. She hadn't been tough and picky to help Leah perfect the tiny details that transformed a good performance into something memorable. No, Alex was right. Diana had been out-and-out jealous of Leah. Leah stopped in her tracks and stared blankly into space. Suddenly she was scared. The prospect of having made such a powerful enemy in the school *and* the company terrified her. Being on Diana's bad side was was far worse than being on Pam's. How could this have happened to her? Leah hadn't done a thing to antagonize the older dancer: all she had done was to be herself and dance.

"Uh, Leah." James slung his arm around her shoulder. "That was a compliment, not some kind of death sentence."

Leah forced herself to smile. Some instinct warned her not to reveal her fears about Diana to James. Leah glanced quickly at her partner. He had shoved up the sleeves of his baggy red sweater and his dark sunglasses masked his eyes. But Leah could feel him staring at her.

She pushed her fears to the back of her mind and, holding out the full fabric of her soft cotton pants, managed a pretty curtsy. "Well, then," she said, "thank you for the compliment. But I'm afraid I have a lot more to learn before I'm ready for any company," she added honestly. And she had a feeling it was more than her dancing she had to master. In the past week she had gotten her first glimpse into the intrigues lurking just behind the romantic facade of the classical ballet world. She sure had a lot to learn in that department. She was beginning to get the picture that not only did she somehow have to rise above it all, as Miss Greene and Madame Preston had told their students, but she'd have to become strong—and smart—enough to survive some pretty destructive treatment by other jealous and more vulnerable dancers.

James guided Leah down the steps and across the parking lot to a cobalt blue Volkswagon. The car surprised her, and Leah reflected that today was full of surprises: the realization about Diana's not very pretty motives for finding fault with her; James's seemingly sincere friendliness. Leah wondered what would be next.

"We dance so much together and we barely know each other," she said, not quite realizing she was speaking aloud.

"That's why we're going to the museum," James said in his usual arch tone.

"So there's a method to your madness," Leah quipped, suddenly feeling manipulated. "It's too much to expect around here that someone's just being friendly."

James stopped and looked at Leah, surprise written all over his face. "You sound kind of mad. Is something wrong?" he asked, his voice full of concern.

Leah colored slightly. "No," she lied. She'd die before she'd admit to James that this whole week had been one rather unpleasant revelation after another. But what did she have to lose? She took a deep breath and said, "It's just that you've never been friendly before." She knew she could tell him that much, but she wasn't about to confide in him her fears about Diana's motivation. She didn't trust him *that* much.

"Hmmm, you did mention that the other night." He gently removed her hand from his arm and began rummaging in his torn canvas duffel for his keys. Leah's eyes bulged. The inside of his bag looked like an overstuffed portable locker. For a moment she stared impolitely at the jumble of towels, sweat bands, socks, tights, T-shirts, and ballet shoes. Were all male dancers closet slobs? James was so fashion-conscious and dressed so neatly. She was shocked at the state of his bag.

James's next words finally diverted her attention. "I didn't know the *real* you until now." James opened the passenger door and peered down at Leah with his intense dark eyes.

"The—the—real me?" she stammered. His response had taken her by surprise. He made their trip to the museum suddenly sound so significant.

James pushed a wayward lock of jet black hair out of his eyes and laughed. "Sure, the part of you that really matters. You have the makings of a great ballerina, Leah." He picked up a stack of records and some sweat socks off the front seat and tossed them into the back of the car.

Leah stood rooted to the spot. She knew she was a really good dancer: lots of people were beginning to tell her that. Miss Greene had always treated her like someone special. But a "great ballerina"? Leah regarded James through narrowed eyes, then climbed into the car. Was he serious? The remote possibility that he was sent a faint thrill up Leah's spine. Then she forced herself to come back to reality. She was a talented first-year student at ballet school. Barring injuries and other unforseeable disasters, she had a very good chance of dancing professionally with a ballet company within the next four years or so. But greatness? Leah reminded herself she had a long, long way to go to even begin to hope for that.

"I'd like to know what makes you tick," said James as if Leah were a girl who walked around shrouded in mystery. Leah enjoyed the picture for a moment, then came back to her senses. She eyed James as he climbed into the driver's seat.

"I don't think I'm the mysterious one in this partnership," she said dryly. She reached up and twiddled a porcelain figurine of Fred Astaire that dangled from the rearview mirror. James rested his hands lightly on the steering wheel and looked at Leah, then threw back his head and laughed. He didn't laugh often, and Leah was shocked by the hearty sound of it.

"Touché, Stephenson," he congratulated her with a grudging note in his voice. "Like everyone else around here, you're probably wondering exactly what makes the 'real' James Cummings tick!"

He had hit the nail on the head and Leah felt she'd been discovered at the scene of a crime. She colored prettily and shrugged. "I want to know why dancing with you feels so right for me, too," she declared, a flirtatious twinkle in her eye. She held her breath waiting for his response. She did want to know why they worked so well together when they danced—when outside of the studio she wasn't sure they had anything in common.

James didn't answer right away. He flicked on the ignition and Fred Astaire began to dance in time to the intense vibrations of the little car. Leah clutched at her stomach and hoped the museum wasn't far. James eased the car into the flow of traffic and said quietly. "I'm from Seattle."

Leah groaned. "I'm from San Lorenzo. Do girl dancers from San Lorenzo and boys from Seattle perform particularly well together?" she teased.

"Maybe." James surprised her with another delighted laugh. "My father's an ex-jock. He was all-American. Coached football at the state university until he had a minor heart attack. My brother's following in his footsteps. I don't see them much. My mother is a housewife—or was until recently, when she decided to open a catering business. I haven't lived at home since I was fourteen."

Leah looked over at James and studied his handsome profile. "You mean you ran away?"

He shook his head. "I moved away." He made it sound like a big difference, but at fourteen moving away and being a runaway sounded pretty much the same to Leah. "I moved to San Francisco to study dance. I lived with Martin Caroli and his wife out in Oakland."

Leah's eyes widened. Martin Caroli was one of the top ballet teachers in the country. He had been on the SFBA staff for a while but preferred coaching professionals, and would fly to Buenos Aires, or Paris, or London on the whim of some of the world's most internationally renowned male and female dancers. The idea that James had studied with him at fourteen impressed Leah immensely.

"When I was ready for SFBA, Caroli sent me to audition."

"I thought boys didn't have auditions."

"We do, though the competition isn't as tough as for the girls. There are, in case you haven't noticed recently in pas de deux class, about four of you to each one of us. And this is the kind of school that attracts boys with scholarships and virtual guaranteed acceptance into the company. Some places the ratio of boys to girls is worse. Anyway, I've been here almost two years now." He looked at Leah and grinned. They were stopped at a light. "That's it. The real life story of James Cummings."

Leah felt curiously disappointed. She certainly knew more about James now than she did an hour ago, but what she knew were the kinds of facts a dancer put on a résumé. She felt James had more to him than where he studied, when, and with whom. She wanted to ask him more about his family, about how he felt when he left home. She wondered why he seemed to have so few friends. She wondered most of all what made it so hard to get to know him. Before she had a chance to ask him more, he launched into a little discourse about his cat. Leah found herself laughing as he told her about finding the kitten the week he moved into the host home he lived in on Jefferson Street. He had tried to hide the cat from Mr. and Mrs. Belvedere, only to discover Mrs. Belvedere feeding the little kitten caviar one night in the kitchen. His cat was orange striped, like Leah's own kitten, Misha, at home. His name was Nijinsky. As they pulled into Golden Gate Park and cruised down Kennedy Drive, Leah realized that James' story about his cat was the most personal thing he had said about himself yet. She admitted to herself that she never expected cool James to be so attached to a pet. She couldn't shake the feeling that beneath James's arrogant exterior lurked a very interesting, if complicated, boy that she would love to get to know.

The traveling Degas exhibit was housed at the De Young Museum. They circled the drive a couple of times before finding a parking place. James locked the car and promised Leah the museum wasn't far.

The day was still mild and the sun still glorious, and then Leah spied the sweeping circular drive in front of the impressive museum building, she only wished their walk could be longer. She slowed down as they approached the entrance, and glanced longingly behind her at the people sprawled on the lawn. She was of half a mind to ask James to forget about the museum. She stretched her arms out wide to catch the breeze and turned in circles around the lawn. She blushed when she realized James was watching her. "I can't help it," she said, clasping her hands, and lifting her face to the slanty rays of the sun. "I haven't been away from the school at all since I've been here. That's over a month now. Every morning I walk half a mile to school; at night half a mile back. I didn't realize how closed in I felt." Leah suddenly felt homesick. She had never lived in a city before. Until this moment she hadn't realized how much she missed the wide expansive vistas of her valley home.

"Closed in at SFBA?" James scoffed, then reminded her sharply, "Where else around here would you get to dance and study with someone like Alicia Preston? All this is nothing compared with really dancing. To really live is to dance." He looked around, a disinterested expression on his handsome face. He cast a disapproving glance at a crowd of teenagers sprawled on the grass having a rowdy picnic.

Leah found herself thinking of Chrissy. Today was Homecoming at San Lorenzo High. By now the football game would be over and Chrissy was probably on her date with her new boyfriend at the beach with the rest of the crowd. Suddenly Leah wondered what doing nothing on Saturday felt like. Ever since she was eight, Saturdays meant dance lessons. Now they meant rehearsals as well as morning class. When the school productions started, they'd mean costume fittings and even more coaching sessions. She cast an envious glance at the picnickers. She'd bet her last dollar that none of these kids had put in a full day's work for love and no pay. Watching them bask in the sun, Leah felt that her life was a little narrow, and she remembered her mother's warning when she was accepted in the school; that choosing a career at fifteen meant giving all this up. Not that she would change it for the world. Still, she wondered how you could really dance, and express those strong, tender emotions, until you had at least a little experience living.

"Oh, James!" Leah gasped a few minutes later when they were inside the museum. They were in a room filled with one colorful Degas painting after another. But Leah was enthralled by only one. She half-ran across the spacious gallery right up to a splendid green and pink pastel drawing of dancers in a nineteenth-century practice studio. "I have this print in my room back home," she exclaimed joyously. "I'm going to bring it back after Christmas. But this one's so much more beautiful." She leaned forward very close until her nose was just inches from the protective glass.

Out of nowhere a security guard appeared at her side. Leah stepped back from the painting and wondered what she'd done wrong. She looked up at his face. He was smiling. She returned his smile with a tentative one of her own.

"Not so close, young lady," he warned in a stern but gentle voice. Then he looked Leah up and down, and his eye traveled to James. He poked his hands in the back pocket of his uniform and rocked back and forth on his heels, his portly stomach sticking way out. "Well, I do say," he announced, grinning at Leah. "If Mr. Degas saw you, he'd paint you straightaway. You're a very pretty young lady. And you're a very lucky young man." He congratulated James.

Leah blushed. She wanted to tell the guard that James wasn't her date. Their visit to the museum was nothing like that. But James squeezed her hand.

The guard went on. "You look just like a ballerina from one of these paintings."

Leah was very red by now. She felt she had to say something. "We're both dancers."

The guard looked from Leah to James and snickered. "A dancer?" He looked James up and down and shrugged.

James's whole body stiffened. Leah glanced sideways at him. His face was flushed. He looked as if he were about to scream.

James grabbed Leah's elbow and abruptly turned his back on the uniformed man. In a couple of long strides he had steered Leah into the next gallery.

"I wasn't finished looking yet!" Leah yanked her arm away. "What was that all about anyway?"

James looked at Leah as if she had just asked the dumbest question in the world.

Quietly she began to seethe.

At least James didn't pretend he didn't know what she was talking about. "I'm sick of it, that's all," he exclaimed darkly. He gave the distant figure of the guard a dirty look and strode to the other side of the room. Leah hurried to keep up with him.

"What exactly are you sick of?" She thought James had been extremely rude and impolite and she wanted to know why.

"Male dancers don't count for a thing—" James

broke off and bit his lip. An angry red color was spreading from his neck onto this cheeks, and his dark eyes sparked fire.

He was really overreacting. Leah's face creased in a puzzled frown. "I can't believe you're so upset because of that guard."

James ran his hands through his hair and looked down at Leah. "I'm sorry, but it ticks me off. Ballet isn't just for girls and in this day and age I can't believe some people are too dumb to realize that. Men like Baryshnikov and Nureyev are household names and still so many guys feel that if you are a dancer you're not a 'real' man. It makes me sick."

"That's changing, James," she told him gently, putting her hand on his arm. His ambition frightened her, and she wanted more than anything to diffuse the charged feeling in the air. James was so angry, she wouldn't be surprised if he went and punched out the guard. "I bet someday that guard will see your picture on the cover of *Newsweek* or *Time* and say, 'Hey, I remember him. He and that little ballet dancer girlfriend of his once looked at a Degas in my museum.'"

Leah's playful comment had the desired effect. James smiled. He patted her hand and bent down and kissed the top of her head lightly. A shiver went down her spine.

She kept her eyes focused on her feet until she felt the blush fade from her cheeks. Then James took her hand and led her into the next gallery, where they smacked straight into Abigail and Pam.

Both girls looked from James to Leah to their

linked hands. Pam's eyebrows shot up. "Hi, guys," she drawled. She grabbed Abigail's arm and steered her into the next room, where the two girls started giggling loud enough for Leah to hear them.

Leah pulled her hand away. "Uh, James," she said, wanting to put as much distance between her and the other girls as possible. "I think it's time to go home. I'm exhausted and starving."

James stared at her as if she were crazy. "Go home? Now?"

Leah half-expected him to ask her out. She colored slightly and couldn't hold back the shy smile that came to her lips. Suddenly she didn't envy Chrissy's date with Otto one bit. And if Pam and Abigail were going to gossip, she'd love giving them something to really gossip about.

"We've got more work to do," James announced, putting his hand firmly under Leah's elbow and leading her to the exit.

"Work?" Leah checked her Betty Boop watch. It was almost six.

"Didn't you understand?" James asked as he started down the winding path that led to the car. "We've got more rehearsing to do. This was just a break. A chance to get to know each other. To make working together even better. I want to get closer to you so our performance will feel more authentic." His voice got low and sexy. "After all, I'm supposed to be Romeo and you're Juliet."

Leah silently cursed the thrill she felt when James said that. She felt so manipulated and confused. "You just asked me out so we'd dance better together?" She was beginning to wonder about James's values. Didn't he care about people as people at all. Was she just a partner—a "perfect partner"—and not a friend, a real flesh and blood girl?

"James," she said decidedly as she slipped into the passenger seat. "I'm not going to go back to school now. Everything's closed down. It's Saturday. I'm supposed to be home. Anyway, I'm tired and I need to eat."

James didn't pay any attention. He passed the turn to Mrs. Hanson's and steered directly down the street leading to the Academy. "Leah, serious dancers don't stop rehearsing because they're tired or hungry. The studio is free tonight, so we'll use it. I don't know about you, but as far as I'm concerned that pas de deux still has some kinks in it. We haven't quite mastered it."

"No, we haven't. And we won't 'master' it before Tuesday. But dancing when you're this tired can't be right, James. And Mrs. Hanson's expecting me for dinner tonight."

"So call her. Tell her you'll be late." When James pulled into the Academy parking lot, it was almost dark.

Leah was tempted to turn around and walk home.

James yanked open the door and reached out his hand for hers. "Leah," he said, gazing down at her with his incredibly soulful dark eyes. "I want us to dance together the way we were meant to. I want to do something beautiful for those high school kids on Tuesday. With a little more work tonight, we'll have a good chance at that."

Leah's better judgment just melted away. When he looked at her like that, it was as if they were dancing together. She had no will separate from his. She grabbed her bag and climbed out of the car. He placed his arm gently around her shoulder, and Leah leaned against him as they headed down the twilight-lit walk into a side entrance to the school.

Chapter 9

Leah changed back into her tights and leotard and phoned Mrs. Hanson from the booth at the head of the hall stairs. Mrs. Hanson warned her not to get too tired or stay too late, then promised to keep something warm and nourishing heating for her on the stove. Hearing her landlady's cheerful voice disheartened Leah. She wanted to be home, hanging out with the other girls, telling them about her afternoon with James. She wanted to be around to counter whatever rumor Abigail and Pam were sure to be starting just about now. She was too tired to be dancing.

James was too tired, too. She knew it even before the second run-through of their program. The magic that had sustained their dancing until now was gone. There was only sweat and grunts and groans and the awful out-of-tune sound of James trying to sing the accompaniment. He had forgotten his tape recorder, and the library was locked, so they'd have to do without one. As he danced he alternately hummed and la-di-dahed the tuneful Prokofiev melody. Leah tried to join in. The both had terrible voices and Leah found it hard to concentrate and sing and dance at the same time. At first she had found it funny. Now she was so tired, singing while she danced felt like trying to walk a tightrope and juggle at the same time.

"James," she finally cried, exasperated, after they had flubbed the same line three times in a row. "This afternoon we were doing this perfectly. Now everything's falling apart." Leah was so wiped out, she felt irritable, annoyed, and about to burst into tears. "Can't we stop now?" she pleaded, grabbing a tissue and wiping the sweat from around her eyes. She sat down on the floor with a thump and stretched her legs out at a 180-degree angle. She flopped forward until her chest was resting on the floor. She lay that way a few moments and then winced. Her right calf muscle was cramping up. She rolled her back up and began massaging the tight spot. Every inch of her body was sore, as if she had been in some sort of drag-out knock-down fight. Her wrists and upper arms were bruised slightly from where James had grabbed her to perform the difficult lifts over and over again. Leah wondered if she'd even be able to stand up again. If they kept this up, she was sure to get hurt. Muscles she didn't even know she had were screaming for her to quit. "Can't we stop before this gets worse?" she begged. Her eyes brimmed with tears.

James was over by the water cooler dousing his head with water. He brushed her comments aside with a wave of his hand. He crumpled a paper cup and tossed it into the trash bin. As he scrubbed the moisture off his face with a towel, he cajoled, "Come on. Just one more time. I know we can do better. Rehearsals always seem to get worse just before a breakthrough."

"Breakthrough!!!" Leah grumbled, "You mean breakdown." Slowly she eased herself back up on her feet. She dangled her head down to the floor and stretched out her lower back. Leah wondered vaguely who put James in charge of this rehearsal. Then she reminded herself she was just a fifteen-year-old first-year student. James was almost a company member. He knew what he was doing—or at least she hoped he did. She took a couple of deep breaths and tried to let her body relax. Then she marched back over to James's side to begin rehearsing the series of turns and slides that had eluded them since the beginning of the session. James started singing. Leah winced at the sound of his voice, but her body mechanically went through the choreography one more time. This time she walked through the steps and didn't dance them.

James stopped singing just long enough to bark sharply at her. "No marking!" Even as he yelled he held the dreamy pose with his left arm out, his left foot pointed well behind him. His weight was over his bent right leg and his eyes were fixed on the mirror. He adjusted the angle of his plié and the tilt of his head until they pleased him, all the time keeping one eye on Leah's reflection as she approached.

Tired as she was, she executed the series of low arabesques and turns full-out. She used the red fire extinguisher hanger in the corner for her spot. Keeping her eyes fixed on the bright object, she executed the complicated combination flawlessly. But her mind wasn't on her dancing at all. She had lost her concentration hours ago and her body was somehow well enough rehearsed to go through the movements no matter where her mind was. At the moment she was wondering if Degas really had known anything at all about real ballet; about how much it hurt and how hard those pretty pink and green dancers really worked and how much sweat there was and how sometimes doing the same step over and over again became relentlessly boring.

"Leah!" James shouted just in time. She had miscalculated her position and almost threw herself into thin air, several feet upstage of James. If he hadn't warned her, she would have fallen into the barre and cracked her head against the mirror.

"Sorry," Leah snapped, and ground the toe of her pointe shoe into the floor. She let out a loud, annoyed breath. She glared at James, then stomped back across the floor with her hands on her hips and shouted over her shoulder. "I guess you want to do it again." Her statement sounded like a challenge.

"Of course. How do you think really great dancers get great?" James asked, completely ignoring Leah's anger. "They work on it until it's perfect."

"Well, maybe I don't want to be a great dancer!" Leah cried willfully, and contemplated marching out of the room and changing her clothes and going home. Then she looked out the window. It was dark, probably past nine, and without James she had no ride.

James didn't respond to her right away. He looked up and spoke to her reflection in the mirror. "I don't care what you want to be," he said in a deliberate voice. "I know I won't stop dancing until I am great. You're my partner—I picked you." He emphasized his last words and met Leah's eyes in the mirror.

Leah felt hurt and bewildered. Why was James attacking her all of a sudden? They had had such a wonderful day together. First the the wonderful rehearsal with Robert earlier, then the trip to the museum. Now he almost seemed to hate her. Leah's lip trembled. If she weren't so tired, she would try to defend herself. Now she just didn't have the energy. "I'm sorry to disappoint you," Leah said in a flat voice. She suddenly wished James would dismiss her, call off the rehearsal and tell Patrick tomorrow he'd dance the pas de deux with someone else.

Then James was by her side. When he spoke, his voice was actually gentle not arrogant at all. "I shouldn't have said that."

Was he actually apologizing? Leah raised her eyes toward his. She didn't know how to respond. James didn't give her a chance to figure it out. He bent down and brushed his lips very gently across her forehead. Leah's pulse fluttered, and she stepped back, confused.

"I forget how new you are to all this." He sounded almost tender. He put his hands on her shoulders and squeezed gently. "I promise we'll go through it only one more time. I know you think I'm working us too hard—"

Leah nodded.

James didn't give her a chance to speak. "It's just that I'm driven, Leah. I'm driven to be the best. I think you are, too. You just don't know it yet. The only way you get to be the best is by working harder than anybody else, the way we're working now."

In spite of her exhaustion, Leah was surprised. Her favorite picture of Fonteyn floated through her mind. Would a great dancer like that give up because she was hungry and tired and it was late on a Saturday night? Leah knit her brow and knew the answer. She let out a sigh and gave in. "Okay, James, one more time." She started across the floor.

"Let's take it from the double tours," he suggested, and Leah's shoulders sagged with relief. Starting with James's short solo meant starting halfway through the piece. Leah was sure she could manage that.

She took a position in the middle of the floor and sang along with James. He began a combination of jetés and turns, circling her, never taking his eyes off her, as she never took her eyes off him. Even so, it happened so fast, she didn't see where she went wrong. One minute he was soaring through the air, his body straight as an arrow whipping around in a crisp perfect double tour.

The next minute he was lying white-faced on the ground, writhing with pain.

Leah was so stunned, for a second she didn't move. Her arm was frozen into a yearning gesture. Then a scream rose from somewhere inside her. "JAMES!!!"

She jumped to her feet and rushed to his side. He was lying flat on the floor with his right leg pulled up to his chest. Leah grabbed his hand. His fingers closed tight around hers. He was squeezing so hard, she thought her bones would break. "James, what happened? Are you okay? What should I do?" she cried, feeling suddenly helpless. She'd never seen anyone get really hurt before in class. A single word formed in her mind. "Help," she murmured. "We need help! HELP!" she screamed at the top of her lungs, then started to her feet. James pulled her down violently beside him. He was shaking his head. "Not help—ice."

"You need more than ice, James." She was on her knees beside him staring at his pale face as if he were mad. For a minute she wondered if he had hit his head and was a little delirious. "James, you need help. You look terrible." With a mighty effort she yanked her hand out of his and got up. She stepped out of arm's reach, and though he grabbed at the hem of her flimsy practice skirt, she avoided his grasp.

He struggled to a sitting position and crossed his injured leg over his other knee. He gingerly pulled off his shoe and sock and delicately rolled up the leg of his stirrup tights. It had only been a few seconds since he fell, but already his right ankle was purple and red. It was an ugly bruise. "Leah, I don't need help. Just get me some ice, fast. Or this is going to swell up so badly, I won't be able to walk on it in the next few minutes, let alone dance." He spoke in a tight, controlled voice.

"James." Leah averted her eyes from his foot. Looking at the bruise was beginning to make her queasy. "We need help. You can't even get down the stairs like that." She started for the door.

"For goodness' sake, Leah, listen to me," he bellowed. "Get ice. Now. There's no time to talk."

Leah agreed with him on that. "Where?" she asked, feeling helpless.

"Downstairs, in the kitchen."

Leah bolted out the door, determined to find some ice. One last look at James's ankle convinced Leah he did need whatever first aid she could come up with as soon as possible. But she was even more determined to find help.

Not until she was halfway down the dimly lit hall did she realize that the school was completely deserted. Only safety lights lit the stairwell and the exit doors. Leah panicked. She groped her way down the shadowy stairs and contemplated calling 911. But an ambulance seemed a little extreme. Maybe if she called Mrs. Hanson's, the boardinghouse, the proprietor could phone her sister, Madame Preston. Surely Madame Preston would know what to do. Instantly Leah dismissed the possibility. She had a funny feeling James and she weren't supposed to be dancing so late on a Saturday night in one of the rehearsal studios. They'd both get into trouble.

Leah made it to the dark cafeteria. With one hand in front of her she finally located the refrigerator. She opened it and the small interior light cast a welcome glow. Leah's hands trembled as she pulled out an ice tray. Before she closed the door she looked around for a towel. She spotted a roll of paper towels over the double sink. She closed the refrigerator and aimed herself in the general direction of the towels. After a moment she secured them. She crept slowly up the back stairs to the top floor.

When she hurried back into the studio, she gasped. James was standing up. He was on one leg, gingerly trying to put some weight on the other.

"Give me that!" he ordered, yanking the ice tray and towels from her hand. Leah stood by helplessly.

"No one was downstairs," she said. "Should I call nine one one, or Diana or someone else on the staff?"

"No way!"

The force of James's reaction made Leah gulp. "But James, I don't even know if I can help you down all those stairs."

"The only help I need right now is a chair." He stared at Leah until she sprang into action.

She pulled the accompanist's stool over toward James and held the ice tray while he applied a cold compress to his ankle. "That must be killing you," she commented, wondering how he could stand the pain.

"It's nothing," he said through clenched teeth.

From the set of his chin and the deep creases in his brow, Leah knew he was lying.

She dropped down to her knees beside him and put the ice tray on the floor. "How are you going to walk on that?"

"I told you, it's nothing to worry about." He sounded almost hysterical.

Leah couldn't understand his reaction. "You don't have to be so defensive," she countered, irritated. She was just trying to help.

"I'm not being defensive." For the first time since he fell he looked into Leah's eyes. He studied her face and seemed to consider his next words carefully before he spoke. "Leah, I don't want—or need—anybody's help. In a few minutes I'll be as good as new."

Leah found his bravado appalling.

James ignored her reaction and went on. "I've had things like this happen before. My right Achilles tendon has been giving me trouble for a while."

Leah frowned and James quickly explained. "It's no big deal. This fall—I landed wrong, I guess—must have made my old injury a little worse."

"James—" Leah started.

"It's *nothing*," he insisted.

Leah folded her hands quietly in her lap and looked down at the floor. She didn't believe James at all. He was in terrible pain and it wasn't just from a bruised ankle bone. Something was wrong with his tendon and as little as Leah knew about injuries, she knew that it was serious. Again she wished she knew James better, that she knew some way to get through his hard head. She thought back on their day together and remembered the only thing that really made an impression on her—he wanted to be a great dancer.

"Not taking care of that now," Leah said as calmly as she could, "means you might get really hurt later, James. You might never dance again."

James's whole body seemed to clench up. He pressed the ice-filled wad of paper towels hard against his ankle and stared at Leah as if she were some kind of enemy. "Don't you even say that. You'll jinx me!" he declared wildly.

"I didn't mean it that way," she cried. "You know I didn't. It's just that you can't ignore being hurt. You're made of flesh and blood, not steel. You aren't Superman; you need help."

James narrowed his eyes and looked at Leah long and hard. "You're overreacting. You're just tired."

"Yeah, right," Leah responded testily. "We should have quit while we were ahead."

"One thing I hate is a girl who says I told you so," James remarked with great disdain.

Leah didn't even bother to respond. She fell silent and wondered exactly how she would get home. She felt like leaving James and his ice pack alone in the empty school. Let someone find him like this tomorrow. For all she cared at that moment, he deserved never to dance again.

When she looked up, James was back on his feet. He was actually walking on his injured foot. He was favoring it, but somehow it was still bearing some of his weight.

"See." He turned around, a smug smile on his

pale face. "I told you it would be good as new. Now, do me a favor and get my things from the changing room. I'll change in here while you get ready. I'd like to get home as soon as possible. Best thing after an ice pack is a very hot bath, and then more ice, and then more heat again. Remember that, Leah," he said with exaggerated sweetness. "This might happen to you sometime."

Leah felt like screaming at him, but she quietly obeyed. She just wanted to get out of there and home.

Halfway to the door he called her back. "And by the way, you don't have to mention this little incident to anyone. Some people might use it as an excuse not to let me dance with you Tuesday. We wouldn't want that, would we?"

"James, are you serious?" Leah threw her hands up in the air. "You won't even be able to walk on that tomorrow. How do you expect to dance by Tuesday? Whether you get help or not, that ankle is really a mess."

"Want to bet?" he challenged as she proceeded into the hall.

She whirled around and replied angrily. "Sure. How much?"

"Five bucks!"

Leah laughed. "That's easy money for me, James." But she wasn't laughing when she finally began to change her clothes. She was desperately trying to make sense out of what had just happened. James seemed ready to risk his whole career because he was afraid to let anyone know he had gotten hurt. Then she remembered something Alex had said the other day after her fall. Something about the school directors not liking their prize dancers sidelined with injuries. Was this one of the awful lessons Leah would have to learn to become a great dancer? That no matter how much pain you were in, the show had to go on? Or rather, that whether you were in it or not, the show would go on without you.

They drove back to the boardinghouse in silence. It was past ten and most of the upstairs windows were already dark when they pulled up. Leah glanced at James out of the corner of her eye. In the glow of the streetlight he looked pale and drawn. Suddenly she felt sorry for him. She put her hand on his wrist and decided to try one more time. "James, you can go to the therapist tomorrow. Maybe Carolyn can help you. Maybe you just need to rest it a few days."

Beneath her hand his arm tightened. Leah sighed with defeat and started out of the car. She was too tired to keep beating her head against a stone wall. So she was startled when James reached for her hand. "I had a nice day," he said, "getting to know you."

Leah looked down at her feet.

"It's nothing, Leah. Dancers always get hurt, and always have to dance on their injuries. Believe me. It's not serious." He affected a light tone. But if it wasn't serious, then why did he sound so afraid?

Leah looked toward the house, and her pulse quickened. Pam Hunter's ground floor window was dark, but the curtain was parted and the bare outline of a face was just visible in the dim light of the street. How long had Pam been there watching them? Leah pulled her hand out of James's and said, "I've got to go in. It's past curfew." She hopped out of the Volkswagen, snagging her stretch pants on the torn upholstery. She didn't care. She just didn't want to give Pam more reason to gossip about her and James.

"Promise me something, Leah." The intensity of James's voice made her turn around. He pulled her back into the car, and her knees folded awkwardly under her on the seat. He cupped her chin in his hand. His dark eyes held hers. A thousand wild horses couldn't have forced her to turn away. It was the same magnetism she felt every time they danced together. The blood suddenly coursed faster through her veins and she grew a little light-headed. She was powerless to resist it. Suddenly his lips brushed hers and Leah heard herself murmur, "Promise you what?"

"Don't mention this to anyone—Alex, Kay—anyone at all. Please." He could have asked her to promise to paint all the white roses in the world red at that moment and she would have agreed.

"I promise," she said as James sealed her promise with another sweet kiss. And Leah didn't care at all that Pam was watching.

Chapter 10

Sunday as usual was a mixed class: company members as well as students showed up. Attendance was optional: many students and dancers chose to skip it. Leah never did. Neither did James. Today's class was special, however. It was Madame Preston's Sunday, the one time a month she took the eleven A.M. class. So today the huge Green Studio was jammed.

Leah found herself across from James at the portable barre that had been set up in the middle of the floor to accommodate the crowd. After last night she couldn't believe he had actually come. His ankle was heavily taped and his white sock bulged slightly. Just standing on it must be agony. That was her first thought. Her second was how calm she felt—calm and distant and very separate from her handsome partner. Last night James had kissed Leah. It was her first real kiss, but she didn't feel romantic as she looked at him now.

She felt a little foolish and embarrassed. No music was playing—in or outside her head. There was no magic. James looked like an ordinary handsome guy with lips set in a pout and his dark complexion unusually wan.

"Are you all right?" she whispered as Madame Preston rapped her hands together sharply. Class was about to start. Leah still expected James to come to his senses and leave.

His body tightened like a spring. He looked over at Leah and glowered at her through his thick dark lashes. "I've never been better," he contended, and continued to stare at Leah until she was forced to look away.

During the first few pliés she could see quite clearly he was really in pain. She kept one eye on Madame Preston, expecting her to stop him any minute. The school's director was so experienced, she must see that James was dancing on a pretty bad injury.

But no one stopped him. Even though the room was cool, beads of perspiration formed on his face and neck before the boys began their strenuous series of turns. James was in terrible pain, Leah could sense it. The same magic that made them dance so well together made Leah ultrasensitive to what he must be feeling—at least physically. She ached for him with every step she took. All the while her mind was repeating the same question. Why was he going through all this just to perform in some dumb high school demonstration? To Leah James's heroics just didn't make sense.

After class the carefree Sunday mood of the dressing room jarred Leah. She didn't say a word as the others made plans for brunch, picnics, and other special weekend activities.

"We're going to Golden Gate Park to ride bicycles!" Kay announced to anyone who would listen.

"Bad for your thigh muscles," Linda warned with a wink at Leah.

Leah returned a halfhearted smile and stared dully into the collection of ragged tutus jamming the clothing rack.

"You should come with us!" Katrina urged, plopping down next to Leah. "Melanie's mother sent a C.A.R.E. package from home and we're going to party afterward on the lawn. Robert told me last night that the good weather's not going to last much longer."

"Stop tempting her, you two!" Alex commanded, giving Leah a worried look. "She's got rehearsal," she added, but continued to stare at her friend. Under the pretext of looking for her boots under the bench, she knelt down next to Leah and whispered, "Is something wrong?"

Leah looked at Alex with glazed eyes. "Rehearsal?" she repeated. She sensed someone's eyes upon her. She looked over her left shoulder.

Diana was staring at her strangely. Leah realized she was half in, half out of her tights and hadn't moved a muscle in the past five minutes. "You and James *do* have rehearsal scheduled, in the East studio upstairs, if I recall." Diana's voice was cool, disinterested, but her eyes were greedily taking in Leah's every gesture.

Diana knows something happened, Leah realized. She quickly finished pulling off her tights. As she rolled them into a little ball, Diana continued to stare at her. Leah turned away and pulled on her T-shirt.

"Why are you changing your clothes?" Diana demanded. Everyone stopped what they were doing to hear Leah's answer.

Leah's eyes widened. She was still facing the wall. She pressed her fingers against her temples and thought frantically for some excuse. She had promised James she wouldn't tell a soul about his injury. Of course they couldn't rehearse today, but what excuse could she possibly fabricate? While part of her tried to manufacture a plausible lie, another part was crying out to tell the truth.

Remembering her fall during the tryouts earlier that week, Leah recalled it was Diana who had been so adamant about not dancing on an injury. That made up Leah's mind for her. Leah couldn't let her strained relationship with Diana get in the way of helping James and preventing what was sure to be a disaster. She'd take Diana aside and explain what was going on. She'd just have to break her promise to James. If he didn't rest his ankle now, something terrible would happen. Leah was as sure of that as she was of her own name.

She turned around and took a deep breath. "Diana"—she began, wishing Pam and all the other girls would just clear out and make her job simpler— "about rehearsal—"

A loud knock on the dressing room door made her jump. Diana frowned. "Who's there?" she asked.

"It's me, James."

Everyone turned around and looked at Leah. She swallowed hard and managed a small smile.

"Is Leah still there?" he asked through the door.

"Yes." Several people answered at once, then giggled. Abigail sniffed loudly, looked pointedly at Leah, and laughed. "He can't stay away from you, can he?"

Another nervous titter went around the room. Pam snickered.

Leah clenched her fist. As she suspected, coming home late last night started the very rumor she wanted to avoid about her and James. "Listen ..." She faced Abigail and started to defend herself. James didn't give her a chance.

"Leah, I'll be warming up in the East studio. Robert's there already. You'd better hurry up." With that James padded down the hall, the sound of his footsteps fading away before Leah could even think of something to say.

"Right," Leah said in a defeated little whisper. "Rehearsal." She sat down heavily on the bench and pulled off her T-shirt. A moment later she was in a fresh pair of tights and her old pale blue leotard. Well, Leah reflected, she had no choice but to go to the East studio and meet him. Maybe face-to-face, in the light of day, she could convince him he was crazy to keep pretending nothing had gone wrong last night. She had to get him to see that to keep dancing was to court disaster— possibly for both of them.

A half hour after Leah knew her instincts were right. In the middle of a shoulder lift, James dropped her and Leah landed hard on her side. In spite of the pain that shot down her arm, she wondered what Robert must be thinking. The accompanist had watched them for days now, dancing this same pas de deux almost flawlessly.

Leah propped herself up on her throbbing arm. "I must be made of rubber!" she joked in a shaky voice. "Nothing broke this time!" James was pacing in a circle, cursing softly to himself. He didn't even say he was sorry.

Robert was standing up behind the piano. "Hey Blondie," he called to Leah, using the nickname he had given her the day she got into the school. "Are you okay?"

Leah felt a surge of warmth rush through her. "Thanks for asking." She gave James a dirty look, but he didn't even notice. He was still pacing, flexing his sore ankle. Leah pressed her lips together. James's usually olive complexion was white with pain.

She hobbled toward the window, tenderly rubbing her bruised ribs. After a moment she laid her forehead against the barre. Lightly she pounded the wooden pole with her fist. Then she straightened up and whirled around, her hands planted firmly on her slim hips. Looking James square in the eye, she delivered her ultimatum. "James Cummings! I've had enough of this."

James took a few menacing steps toward her, his expression dark.

Before he could say a thing, Robert was between them. The skinny pianist poked his glasses up on his nose and grinned. "I think we all need a break. Leah took quite a fall there. She needs to catch her breath. I'm going to get some coffee downstairs. Anybody want anything?"

James's shoulders tightened noticeably. "You're not in charge of this rehearsal," he started to protest, then looked at Leah. He narrowed his large dark eyes and let out a slow breath. "But you're right." James paused to flick a lock of hair out of his eyes. "A break would do us all good. Leah and I have some business to discuss." Before Robert was even out of the room, James had Leah by the elbow. He pulled her forcibly over to a corner and pressed her against the wall.

Leah yanked her arm away. "What are you doing?" She rubbed her upper arm gingerly. Her skin was blossoming with angry red marks where James had grabbed her.

James returned her question with one of his own. "What are you trying to do today?"

"What am *I* trying to do?" Leah laughed uneasily. She glanced around the empty room. She suddenly wished Robert hadn't left them alone.

"No," James said, and stomped away a little. Leah carefully worked her way out of the corner. Some instinct prompted her to put some distance between her and James. "The real question is what are you trying to prove?"

Leah shook her head and wondered if James was going crazy.

"Don't look so innocent, Leah," he snarled. "Just because I wouldn't listen to your dumb advice last night and give in to this silly problem with my ankle, you're trying to prove that I can't dance on it. You've been screwing up my timing all afternoon."

"I've been screwing up *your* timing?" Leah tugged down the back of her leotard with an angry yank and snorted with disgust. "You are the most stubborn, crazy boy I've ever met. The reason we've been having such a bad time today— and don't forget you're the one who just dropped me—" Leah's voice was rising with every word. James glanced nervously at the door and Leah looked up at the ceiling in disgust. She lowered her voice and continued in a tight, angry whisper. "The reason this rehearsal has been such an absolute disaster is that you are in pain. You keep favoring that dumb foot of yours and of course you're off balance."

James threw his head back and laughed darkly. "Now she tries to tell me she knows how my foot is feeling," he said to the empty room. He looked scornfully back down into Leah's angry eyes. "Tell me, Blondie"—he imitated Robert's voice with great derision—"are you psychic? Can you read minds?"

Before Leah could answer, he turned away abruptly. He stepped on his foot wrong, and his leg buckled out from under him. "Ahhh!" A loud exclamation of real pain filled the room.

Leah dropped down instantly by his side. "Oh, James," she begged, her eyes bright with sympathetic tears. "Won't you listen to me? You can't dance like this. I'm sure if you visit the physical therapist and get a week's rest you'll be fine." She tried to sound reasonable, but her heart was pounding. His foot was obviously even worse than last night. Last night walking on it didn't hurt him half as bad as today. Class had made it worse. And then rehearsal. By Tuesday ... Leah shuddered to think of the condition James would be in then. And they would be dancing in front of an audience on a stage. What if he fell? What if he dropped her then? What if she got hurt? With each question Leah pulled back a little from James. She took her hand off his arm and instantly knew what to do.

She jumped up and started, half-running to the door. "I'm going to get help," she said with great force.

Somehow James scrambled to his feet. He limped heavily but quickly toward her, grabbed her arm, and held her hard. "You're not going anywhere. You promised," he reminded her, but his reminder sounded more like a threat.

"Don't talk to me that way!" Leah cried, furious. She tried to pull her arm away, but this time James was holding her far too hard. "You're hurting me!"

"If you take one more step toward that door, if you go to anyone for help, if you dare breathe a word of what happened last night to anyone—" He paused and shook her hard. "You'll really be hurting. Understand that?" he threatened her.

Leah went white. Her heart was thumping so hard she though she would faint. James dropped her arm and continued to stare at her. She should have run then, but James started talking. Leah couldn't believe what he was saying.

"Don't you understand anything, Stephenson?" he asked bitterly. "You were born with a silver spoon in your mouth. Everything comes easy to you." James limped away and walked over to the window. Leah stood next to him at the barre and watched him carefully as he spoke. "When I was just a kid—six, seven, who knows—I saw a film of Nureyev. I wanted to dance like that. Just like that. Everyone in my family laughed at me. So I sneaked off every day after school to a local ballet teacher. She gave free lessons to boys because no boys in my neighborhood wanted to study dance. When the other guys in my class found out, they were really mean to me. They called me a girl."

Leah closed her eyes and felt James's pain. She knew boys had trouble trying to study ballet. In big cities they could manage somehow, but often they were teased to death, until they quit. She looked with renewed interest at James. She pictured him as a little boy, wanting to dance so badly that not even losing every one of his friends could keep him from his dream. An acute stab of sympathy pierced her heart. Leah realized she suddenly understood something very important about him.

"But I knew what I wanted to do," he reminisced, sounding almost dreamy. Then he shook his head and faced Leah again. "It's all I want to do now. I was born to dance," he declared with great vehemence, "and no one will stop me!" A threatening note crept back into his voice.

Leah forced herself to stay calm. "I don't want to stop you from dancing," she explained as gently as she could. "I want you to get better so that you can go on dancing. You could get hurt even worse, James." Her voice, her eyes, pleaded with him to understand and be reasonable.

James scoffed at her openly. "You really don't get the picture, do you?" His voice shook slightly. He balled one hand into a fist and drove it into his other palm. He leaned heavily back against the barre and looked up at the ceiling as he spoke. "Around here—around any school, in any company, really—there are hordes of people coming up behind you."

Leah's body tensed. She knew what James was going to say next and she didn't want to hear it. Alex had said the same thing a couple of days ago—that new dancers were always coming up in the ranks, making older star students like Alex look a little less lustrous; threatening the careers of dancers already in the company. Leah hated that picture and wished James would just shut up.

"Every one of them just dying to get your part, do your bit. If you miss a performance, chances are someone else will come in and do a better job—"

Leah couldn't let him go on. "That's ridiculous. There are no hordes of male dancers trying to compete with you. No guy in this school is as talented as you." She couldn't believe she actually said that out loud. A few days ago she would have died rather than bolster what she had thought James's indestructible ego.

He acknowledged her compliment with a terse

laugh. "Thanks, but that's not the point. If no one better is here today, they might be around tomorrow or the day after. Or say someone better isn't just over the horizon—then there's surely someone who doesn't get injured, who's more dependable, who the company can count on." He stopped and stared at Leah.

She was fiddling with a thread dangling from a hole in her leotard. Her face was pale. Obviously every word James was saying was sinking in.

"I see you're beginning to get my drift," he commented after a moment. "So now you know why I can't give in. I've worked too hard to get where I am." He paused and slammed his fist into his hand again, and a bright, expectant expression crossed his face. "Next year my life really begins. I'll be in the company. Diana said I might get some solo roles. I'll get reviews. Oh, Leah," he cried, suddenly turning around. The anger in his face was gone. He looked so incredibly happy, Leah thought her heart would break. "Leah, my dream will finally come true." He stared at her as if there had been no angry words between them. His voice was honest and wistful as he said, "I just wish you weren't fifteen. You're the real partner I was born to dance with. We're made for each other." He reached out. Leah recoiled slightly as he took her arm. He turned her around and made her face the mirror. Her blonde head came right to his shoulder. She was so fair, he was so dark. They did look wonderful together.

"Maybe in a couple of years we'll be able to perform professionally together," he said wistfully.

Leah almost got lost in his fantasy. The sound of Robert's footsteps on the stairs outside jolted her back to reality. "James——" she started.

James had heard Robert approaching, too. He tightened his hold on Leah's shoulder and forced her to face him. "Remember, Leah, you are not to breathe a word of this to anymore. I'll manage to dance Tuesday. Don't you worry about that. And I won't drop you again. I'm not going to hurt you." He paused for a long, deliberate moment. When he spoke again, the expression on his chiseled face was almost cruel and very threatening. "Unless you spill the beans."

Leah nodded mutely. She didn't promise aloud. She couldn't. She was too scared. Then Robert walked in, balancing his coffee in one hand and a half-eaten jelly doughnut in the other.

Managing not to limp, James approached the pianist with a smile. "We decided to break for today. We're both a little overworked."

Robert looked from Leah to James and nodded. "You're sure?" he asked, puzzled.

"We're sure," Leah heard herself answer.

"Well, as I said to Diana the other day, you two don't need half the work she said you did. You dance—usually—" he added with another puzzled look at Leah, then James, "as if you were made for each other."

Chapter 11

*The royal blue San Francisco Ballet Academy van sped smoothly across the Golden Gate Bridge into Marin Country. Kay was sitting up front next to the twenty-five-year-old driver, Raul Zamora. The dark-haired, mustached young man was high on Kay Larkin's list of favorite people, and Leah could understand why. The director of San Francisco's Teatro Hispánico worked part-time at the Academy to help support his struggling theater enterprise, and he was as friendly, warm, and outgoing as the Philadelphia girl herself. Everyone teased Kay mercilessly, saying she had a crush on Raul. Even now Alex was making some pretty pointed remarks, which Kay happily let sail right over her head.

Usually Leah would join in just for the fun of prodding Kay into some reaction. But it was Tuesday and the crowded van's destination was Kentfield Regional High and the year's first dance* demonstration. She wasn't in the mood for jokes. Even if she wanted to join in the general banter, James wouldn't let her. He had virtually forced her into the corner of the backseat and was sitting very close, his arm clasped tightly around her shoulder. He was mostly looking out the window, but he kept his head very close to hers. His behavior was having the exact effect he intended, and Leah was fuming inside because of it: Diana, Patrick, and the cast of students were leaving them alone, excluding them from all conversation, and smiling knowingly in their direction from time to time. James was making it perfectly clear that something intense and romantic was going on between them.

Leah knew it was all a farce. She knew he wanted to keep her away from the other kids in case she was suddenly tempted to break her promise and announce to the world that he was about to dance on a foot any normal human being could barely walk on.

"Don't look so scared, Leah," he whispered into her ear. Leah wanted to pull away but there was no space. She was already squashed against the door.

"I'm not scared," she muttered in reply. She fiddled with her loosely plaited braid and began to pray that nothing awful would go wrong today.

"The doctor gave me a cortisone shot in my ankle," he announced blithely.

Leah snapped her head around and stared at him with wide blue eyes. "You went to Carolyn?"

she asked loudly. Several heads turned around at the mention of the school therapist's name. Alex's eyes were full of questions as she met Leah's glances.

James silenced Leah with a threatening look. Leah sighed with frustration. "No," he said in a low, harsh whisper. "To a doctor in town. Some dancer gave me the address ages ago. He specializes in dance and sports medicine. He gave me this shot this morning and told me I'd be fine today."

Somehow Leah doubted those were the doctor's exact words, but as she scrutinized James more carefully, she realized he did look better. The color was back in his cheeks and he didn't look as if he were in pain. Still, she couldn't help reminding him he had just broken one of SFBA's primary rules and regulations: no outside medical treatment for dance injuries without consultation from Academy medical staff. Alex had explained to them all one night that the rule wasn't just for insurance purposes; it was to keep an eye on young dancers to be sure they didn't start really mistreating their bodies.

James didn't want to hear a word of it. They spent the rest of the trip in silence. James kept his hand firmly on Leah's shoulder and closed his eyes, pretending to sleep. She knew he was just faking it, because every time she looked at him, his eyes met hers from under half-closed lids, and she turned away, defeated. It was probably too late to tell anyone about James's injury anyway.

Leah felt angry and helpless, as if she were being held hostage to James's impossible dreams.

Leah was grateful for the commotion in the corner of the girl's locker room that had been curtained off for a dressing room. The complicated business of makeup in such crowded quarters with bad lighting and the smallest of hand mirrors took her mind off James and the awful churning in the pit of her stomach.

"Do you believe they had to put Coke on the floor of the stage?" Kay wailed from the corner. "And Patrick decided not to use the curtain. He said it would be fun for the students to get a behind-the-scenes view of what goes on backstage before a ballet begins." A chorus of groans met her announcement. Kay and the other "Barre Belles" merely had to don clean practice clothes, with fairly spotless pointe shoes. Though they were just demonstrating a fairly difficult but ordinary ballet class, their makeup had to be pretty heavy because of the stage lights.

"Coke makes the floor sticky," Diana explained, trying to calm everybody down. "Auditorium stages have the worst floors to dance on. You'd think they made slick on purpose to try the patience of visiting dance companies."

Diana was dressing in a spot right near Leah. The bodice of her costume was still unzipped and she looked at Leah over her shoulder. "Zip me up, hon!"

Leah stared at the ballerina in disbelief. She hadn't been alone with Diana since that first rehearsal with James, but her impression had been they weren't on very friendly terms. "Uh, sure," she said, trying to keep her hands from trembling. When she finished, she smoothed out the gorgeous red tulle of the short tutu. Diana and Patrick were dancing the flashy pas de deux from *Don Quixote*. Madame Preston was teaching Leah and Pam the girl's tricky fan variation in coaching class. If it hadn't been for her fears about James and her awful case of stage fright, Leah would be looking forward to seeing Diana and Patrick close the show this afternoon. She hadn't seen the pas de deux performed in costume yet and knew Diana had just the right technique and flair to perform the variation brilliantly. "All done," Leah said lightly, brushing a piece of white fluff from Pam's *Sylphides* costume off the black velvet trim of Diana's bodice.

Diana didn't thank her, but turned around and checked out Leah's costume. "Take care of this!" she commanded possessively. She tugged the sheer flimsy gown down farther on Leah's chest and straightened one of the twisted glittery shoulder straps. Then she zipped Leah up and frowned. "It's a bit tight for you, isn't it?"

"Mrs. Howard said it was a perfect fit," Leah said as nicely as she could.

"Well, maybe you've gained some weight. You'd better watch it." Diana gave Leah a light smack on her rear, and walked away.

Leah wanted to scream, but she never had the chance. Patrick was banging on the locker room door. "Hey, girls, it's time to start. Get out here and start warming up."

Leah grabbed the hair spray and coated her thick blond hair well. Before they set out for Kentfield, Madame Preston had given all the girls a lecture about performance penalties. Though they were just students, and this was just a high school performance, it counted. They were to be treated like professional dancers, which meant they could be fined. Penalties would be levied if a wisp of hair was seen straggling out of their buns, if their toe shoe ribbons weren't perfectly smooth or came undone, or if their costumes fell off. Everyone giggled at that, until Madame told of an opening night performance of the Royal Ballet some years back in New York. Dead center on the stage of the Metropolitan Opera House, during a performance of *The Nutcracker*, the company's leading ballerina's skirt came undone during a supported turn. Her partner ripped the dangerously trailing garment off her waist and tossed it into the wings. But the ballerina had to finish the entire adagio section of a grand pas de deux in a skimpy leotard and tights. No one giggled when Madame Preston told them the amount the internationally famous star was fined.

Leah was still warming up in the shallow wings when the "Barre Belles" went on. Patrick had choreographed even the warm-up period, with the boys and girls chatting to one another and doing their floor stretches right onstage. When they went to the barre, Patrick, from his spot on the top of the steps leading down from the stage, picked up a microphone and described the name and purpose of each exercise. Leah hadn't had a chance to see Kay or Alex or the other students rehearse, so she found herself enjoying their performance and actually learning something from it. Patrick was a born showman, and Kay proved to be a willing and very funny stand-up comic. She threw her heart into demonstrating what could go wrong with each step. She didn't even mind falling flat on her bottom with her legs splayed out to show how one didn't land from a complicated jump. Leah was shocked Kay didn't get hurt, and couldn't help but crack up with the audience at the startled ridiculous expression Kay mugged for the crowd.

Her warm-ups finished, Leah tugged on her leg warmers and watched the boys' demonstration with great interest. Alex had certainly pegged each boy's strength perfectly. Kenny, too short and square to ever be a premier danseur, brought the house down with his extraordinary elevation and daring turns midair. Michael executed a complicated series of turns in second. Though he wasn't much to look at, he had the carriage and regal bearing of a true danseur noble, a real ballet prince. In a couple of years he'd be quite a presence onstage. As Leah watched him, she regretted that Michael hadn't been cast as her Romeo. Michael was too sensible and considerate to dance on an injury.

While Pam prepared to go on for her solo, Patrick discussed the qualities that made a good male dancer. Leah was surprised at the comments and questions from the audience. Suddenly she wished this were San Lorenzo High and she did know the kids. She had never dreamed they'd be so receptive to the SFBA program.

Leah stared across the empty stage into the wings and spotted James. Her heart stopped. He looked wonderful in Romeo's soft full shirt. It was cut low and hung open in the front and the sleeves billowed romantically with every move he made. He was holding on to the back of a chair performing a series of loose-swinging battements en cloche. His movement was free and easy and he didn't seem to be in pain at all. Leah relaxed slightly. He looked fine. Maybe that doctor was right. The shot seemed to have helped James, though Leah couldn't believe one single injection of a drug could cure an injury like his. But hope surged through her. Maybe he would actually make it through this performance.

Pam was on next. Leah, spellbound, watched her rival's extraordinary jump. The mazurka from *Les Sylphides* showed off Pam's strong technique to great advantage. In spite of herself, Leah found herself clapping heartily with the other girls in the wings. Then Pam brushed past, her nose up in the air and her cheeks flushed with exertion and pride. Leah met her eyes and couldn't help but return Pam's triumphant smile. She looked so proud and happy.

"That was great!"

Pam's finely penciled brows shot up and her smile tightened. Nevertheless, she actually sounded civil as she said, "Thank you." Pam fluffed out her tutu and ran back on stage for a bow. "Break a leg."

Leah's blood ran cold. She reminded herself Pam didn't mean anything nasty by that. It was standard theater jargon for "good luck." Pam had no way of knowing about James's foot.

Leah forced her mind back on the here and now. In less than a minute she'd be dancing with James. There was no time left to worry about falling or being dropped. Leah tugged off her leg warmers, grateful for the extra time Pam's curtain call gave her to warm up. She tuned out the hoots and whistles rising from the boys in the audience and felt her own body grow more limber as she softly descended into a deep plié.

Then Patrick took the microphone and stepped back onto the side apron of the spacious stage. "Now we have a pas de deux—a love duet if you will—" Patrick paused and smiled as the expected titter rippled through the audience of girls and boys. "Pas de deux—or double work—is the real high point of classical ballet. Two people dancing together as if they are made of one body—or at least giving the illusion of being one body— provides the most beautiful and technically challenging opportunities for even the seasoned professional dancer. Today's pas de deux, from *Romeo and Juliet,* will be danced by students, not professionals. They are both about your age, and the age of the hero and heroine, whose tragic love story they are about to portray. I'd like to present Leah Stephenson and James Cummings in the balcony scene from the Bay Area Ballet's new production of Prokofiev's *Romeo and Juliet.*"

The stage lights blacked out and Leah stepped cautiously out of the wings. A dab of fluorescent tape marked her starting point on the floor. Her heart was pounding and her legs felt as limp as overcooked noodles. Her mind suddenly went completely blank. She couldn't remember the opening move, the first step. She couldn't remember exactly where James would be when the lights came up. And then she remembered James's foot. What if he couldn't catch her for the opening lift. She turned around to the wings. The first face she saw was Pam's. Behind her Diana was watching with narrowed eyes. Leah swallowed hard and turned around again. It was too late. What would happen with James would happen. She reminded herself that this was just a high school demonstration. These were just kids in the audience, not critics, not people who really knew the art of ballet.

A moment later someone flipped on the tape recorder and the music began. Two spotlights fell in perfect circles, isolating her and James from the darkness. She heard girls in the front row gasp. She was relieved that her body seemed to have a memory of its own. She slowly raised her head and arm in a yearning, searching gesture, a gesture she had repeated at least a hundred times during the past week. When she saw James opposite her, she smiled. No wonder those girls had gasped. Charisma oozed from him. He looked like a dream come true, like every young girl's Romeo, incredibly handsome with his dark hair falling over his forehead and his eyes enormous with ardent love.

Leah performed the first halting steps to the dance, then, pretending to finally recognize her Romeo, she sped diagonally across the floor toward him, her thin costume flowing behind her like the wind, her beautifully pointed feet barely skimming the surface of the stage. His hand clasped hers with a sure, strong grip and the familiar magical feeling surged through her. But when she jumped into the first lift, she could feel his arm shaking as he held her over his head. The dreamy expression froze on her face.

"Don't worry," he said in a loud whisper. "I'll be okay." No one but Leah could hear him over the loud passionate music.

Then she was back down on the ground. Her mind was a blur of terrible frightened thoughts. What would she do if he dropped her? What if she couldn't get up again? But her body kept going through the motions of the dance, and suddenly Leah understood why dancers rehearsed so much, doing the same steps again and again and again. Because though the magic was gone, and she couldn't think about what to do next, her body had found a wisdom of its own.

Time and music flashed by so fast, the piece was half over before Leah realized it. She found herself kneeling center stage on the floor, catching her breath as she stretched each arm in turn in yearning gestures toward James. He had begun his difficult solo. But something was wrong. Leah knew that even before the gasp went up from the wings. Leah was looking one way and James was circling her in the opposite direction, the wrong direction. Alex hissed her name from the wings to get her attention. Then Leah realized. James had changed the choreography. He had planned it out so he wouldn't have to land from any of his tours en l'air on his injured right foot. Leah kept smiling but cursed between her closed lips. She quickly adjusted her position and hoped none of the kids watching would notice she had been looking yearningly into blank space while Romeo was dancing somewhere behind her back.

The tough turns began and Leah held her breath. To her amazement James had changed the steps completely: he had substituted far more difficult turns that landed on one foot rather than two. She was glad she couldn't see the expression on Patrick's face. That a student had changed the choreography in the middle of a performance was unthinkable. Leah knew famous dancers did it often to show off their strong points and to avoid having to do turns to their weaker side. But James had no claim to fame yet, and Leah was suddenly afraid for him.

But the audience couldn't have cared less. The didn't know what he was doing. Cheers resounded through the auditorium as James executed one more difficult turn midair after another, always landing on his left foot.

Leah relaxed a bit as she realized that James had gotten through the bad part without getting hurt. He finished the flamboyant variation and went right into a ballet run that was supposed to end in her arms. It was an easy step, so Leah wasn't prepared when James collapsed in a heap on the floor at her feet.

Diana cried out from the wings. Leah's hand flew to her mouth. Then someone turned the music off. A puzzled murmur rippled through the audience. One of the girls in the front row screamed. Leah scrambled to her feet and hurried to James's side. His eyes were closed and his handsome features were contorted in pain.

She tried to call his name, but no sound came out of her throat. She looked around desperately for help. Some voice inside said the show must go on. Whoever made that up, she thought, was crazy. How could anything go on with James lying at her feet?

Then the curtain dropped. The whole cast flooded the stage. Diana pushed Leah aside brusquely and bent over James. Someone helped her to her feet and threw a shawl around her shoulders. Leah stood there shaking, unable to take her eyes off the terrible sight of James as he lay crumbled like an oversize rag doll on the floor.

"James!" Diana cried, a note of fear in her voice. The ballerina rubbed his wrists and shook his shoulder. He didn't move. She whirled around and confronted Leah, her lovely face distorted with anger. "What has he been doing? Drugs? What?" She was almost screaming at Leah, as if whatever had happened were Leah's fault. Leah couldn't answer. She hadn't heard a word Diana said.

"Stop it!" James whispered hoarsely, and tried to sit up. His face whitened as he tried to prop himself up on his elbows. "It's not Leah's fault." His voice was weak and each sentence he spoke seemed to come only with great effort. "My Achilles tendon. The right foot. The cortisone wore off, I guess. I don't think I can walk."

He fell back in a dead faint.

Chapter 12

On the other side of the curtain Patrick made an announcement to the audience. Leah could hardly believe his crazy promise that in a few minutes the show would continue. A moment later he was standing center stage. With a sharp clap of his hands, the hysterical babble died down and he took charge.

Kay guided Leah to the wings and got her a glass of water. Alex peeled of her own leg warmers and shoved them into Leah's hands. "Put these on. You'll have to keep warm."

Mechanically Leah obeyed. Then Patrick and Michael came by and stood on either side of James, helping him hop painfully toward the stairs leading to the boys' changing room. As they passed Leah, James stopped. He reached out his hand toward her. "I'm sorry," he said, his eyes moist with tears. "I should have listened to you." He squeezed her hand. It wasn't a very strong squeeze.

As he disappeared down the steps, a cry rose up from Leah's throat and she burst into loud, uncontrollable tears.

Kay's arm was around her instantly. "Oh, Leah," Kay murmured, holding her tight. "He'll be okay."

Leah shook her head dismally and sobbed. "It's all my fault." She sank down in the chair Kenny had brought for her, and wept as though her heart were breaking. "It's all my fault," she sobbed again and again.

"You'd better explain yourself." Diana had walked up. Her voice was as sharp as broken glass. The girls around Leah and her friends backed off.

Kay stayed by her, rubbing her cold hands. Alex stood with one hand on the back of Leah's chair, stroking her hair.

Leah shook her head ruefully. She finally glanced up, her eyes swollen and red, her heavy stage makeup streaked with rivers of tears. "I should have told you. I knew I should have gone to somebody but—I didn't—and what—" She could barely get the next terrible words out. "What if he never dances again?" The expression of pain on James's face was so horrible that Leah couldn't imagine he'd ever recover.

"Don't be ridiculous," Alex said forcefully. Leah just cried harder.

"What should you have told me?" Diana asked in a cold, controlled voice. Leah looked up sharply. The ballerina was furious.

"That James got hurt Saturday night." There, Leah had done it. She had broken her promise. It didn't matter now. It was all too late.

"Go on!" Diana commanded, tapping her foot. The box of her shoe made a hollow sound on the sticky floorboards.

"We were dancing and he fell doing one of his double tours and I wanted to get help," Leah said in a broken voice. "I really did." The tears started up again, but Leah forced herself to continue. She didn't want to hold anything back now. She deserved whatever punishment was coming to her. She had risked James's career because she was too scared to do what she knew was right.

"So why didn't you call someone?" Kay asked softly.

"Because he wouldn't let me. He told me—he told me that if I mentioned his injury to anyone— he'd—" Leah shuddered at the memory. "He'd hurt me." Then she remembered the exact sequence of events. "He told me that Sunday when we tried to rehearse again and he dropped me, and Robert left the room to take a break."

Diana spurned Leah's explanation. "James is the most promising dancer in the whole Academy. If he really can't dance again and—" Diana stopped herself and looked disdainfully at Leah. In a low, measured voice only Leah could hear she said, "James was about to be signed up as my partner next season. If you've ruined that ..." She left her threat unspoken. Leah's head snapped up. The pieces of the puzzle fell into place. Diana wasn't just jealous because Leah was a promising young dancer, but because she danced so perfectly with James. And soon everyone in the school and company would have noticed that. No wonder Diana hated her.

"Don't look at me like that!" Diana bellowed. She considered Leah carefully. "So are you going to tell us what really happened? James Cummings would never threaten you. Admit it!" she commanded.

"Yes, he would!" Alex stated quickly. "I know he would, and I know him better than anybody around here." She looked at Pam, Katrina, Linda, and Diana in turn. No one argued with her. "He won't let anything come between him and his dancing. He has these crazy ideas that if he isn't perfect all the time, if he isn't always 'on,' he's not going to make it as a dancer. I tried to get through to him about a hundred times. I told him he was overdoing it way before he started rehearsing with Leah. He couldn't—or wouldn't—hear anything about it. This was bound to happen sooner or later. He's obsessed."

Leah was crying more quietly now. She didn't notice when Patrick walked up. But at the sound of his firm, gentle voice, she looked up. She wondered how much he had already heard. She waited for him to say something, to tell her to get out of there, to go back to the school, pack her things and go home. Or maybe he'd just send her straight to Madame Preston. Leah's heart ached as if it were breaking. She hadn't thought her dreams would come to this.

Patrick cleared his throat. "We'll talk about this more later, back at school. At the moment we have a performance to finish."

Leah stared stupefied at Patrick. Was he serious? This wasn't a real show. Everyone was too shaken to go on. The kids out front would understand that.

"Right." Diana straightened up. She was still angry. Leah could see it in her eyes, but she was also a highly professional, disciplined dancer. She turned toward Leah, her voice firm and not completely hostile as she said, "Get out of that costume."

Without thinking, Leah stood up and began fumbling for her zipper.

Patrick grabbed her arm. He spoke directly to Diana "She's got to finish."

"Finish?" The shock of it dried the tears in Leah's eyes. "How can I finish?" she asked in a squeaky voice.

"You all certainly can figure out how to dance a pas de deux without a guy, can't you?" Pam drawled sarcastically. One look from Alex and Pam shut her mouth.

"I don't know it well enough yet," Michael said, nervously wrapping a towel around his fingers, then unwrapping it again. He flashed Leah an apologetic look, then wiped the beads of perspiration off his brow.

"Of course not," Patrick assured him in a calm voice. "I'll finish the pas de deux with Leah."

"Patrick, have you lost your mind?" Diana glared at her colleague. She whipped Leah around and began to undo her costume herself. Leah stood there limp, not helping her, not trying to stop her. "Obviously you're the only male dancer here who can do it. And obviously, this girl"—she gave Leah a not very gentle shake—"is not in any condition to continue her performance. Look at her. She's in shock. Poor kid. This is her first time dancing in public with a partner and this happens. You must be nuts."

Leah was stepping out of her costume, too confused to remember to feel embarrassed by the boys still standing in the wings, when Patrick spoke up again. "Put that back on," he practically yelled. "You're not in charge of this gig, Diana." He turned on the ballerina. "I am. Leah has to go on again, right now. That's the name of the game ... and you know it," he concluded with a significant lift of his eyebrows.

Diana held her ground a minute, then shrugged as if she couldn't care less. "Okay, let her make a fool of herself. Poor kid," she repeated, her voice dripping sympathy. "I don't envy her one bit."

Alex helped Leah back on with her dress and pulled some powder out of her bag to begin touching up Leah's ruined makeup. The whole time Alex worked on her, Leah stared at Diana. Diana had called her a poor kid, but she hadn't meant it at all. She was probably glad this had happened to Leah—as long as there was a chance James would dance again.

Leah couldn't take her eyes off Diana. Everything Alex and James had said began to make sense. The pieces of Diana's story fell into place. Diana was afraid of her coming up behind her in the ranks of the company. To Leah, being an apprentice with the Bay Area Ballet seemed a lifetime away. But it wasn't. Diana realized that.

Leah's head was spinning. Diana had planned on building a whole career with James as her brilliant new partner. But James had preferred working with Leah. And Diana was jealous of her for that. Diana was jealous of Leah's dancing, period. She was afraid Leah would step into her roles some day, into her position in the company, as easily as Leah stepped into her costume now. She must be a pretty good dancer to scare the gifted Diana Chen that much.

And someday Leah would be in the same position, with a new younger girl coming through the ranks behind her.

All at once she knew what she had to do. If she didn't go on again now, Diana would win some kind of subtle battle in a war Leah had found out about only a few days ago. And Leah would lose ground as a person and as a dancer because she would not have met the challenge and tried to do what was required of her. When a ballerina went onstage, she had to be prepared for any emergency. Her job was to bring some beauty and grace into the lives of her audience. Today Leah's job was still only half done.

The determination in her voice amazed her as she said, "Patrick, I'll need some time to warm up again. In a minute I'll be ready to go on." As she spoke, her hands stopped shaking and she was finally able to force the pale vision of James out of her mind. After the performance there'd be plenty of time to think about him, to see what she could do to help, to figure out exactly where and why she went wrong. Facing Madame Preston was going to be rough. There was bound to be a strict penalty for shielding James the way she had. But she couldn't allow herself to think about that now.

Now it was time to dance, and to Leah Stephenson that was all that really mattered in the end.

GLOSSARY

Adagio. Slow tempo dance steps; essential to sustaining controlled body line. When dancing with a partner, the term refers to support of ballerina.

Allegro. Quick, lively dance step.

Arabesque. Dancer stands on one leg and extends the other leg straight back while holding the arms in graceful positions.

Assemblé. A jump in which the two feet are brought together in the air before the dancer lands on the ground in fifth position.

Ballon. Illusion of suspending in air.

Barre. The wooden bar along the wall of every ballet studio. Work at the barre makes up the first part of ballet class.

Battement. Throwing the leg as high as possible into the air to the front, the side, or the back.

Bourrée. Small, quick steps usually done on toes. Many variations.

Brise. A jump off one foot in which the legs are beaten together in the air.

Centre work. The main part of practice; performing steps on the floor after barre work.

Chaîné. A series of short, usually fast turns on pointe by which a dancer moves across the stage.

Corps de ballet. Any and all members of the ballet who are not soloists.

Developpé. The slow raising and unfolding of one leg until it is high in the air (usually done in pas de deux, or with support of barre or partner).

Echappé. A movement in which the dancer springs up from fifth position onto pointe in second position. Also a jump.

Fouetté. A step in which the dancer is on one leg and uses the other leg in a sort of whipping movement to help the body turn.

Jeté. A jump from one foot onto the other in which the working leg appears to be thrown in the air.

Mazurka. A Polish national dance.

Pas de deux. Dance for two dancers. ("Pas de trois" means dance for three dancers, and so on.)

Piqué. Direct step onto pointe without bending the knee of the working leg.

Plié. With feet and legs turned out, a movement by which the dancer bends both knees outward over the toes, leaving the heels on the ground.

> *Demi plié.* Bending the knees as far as possible leaving the heels on the floor.

Grand plié. Bending knees all the way down letting the heels come off the floor (except in second position).

Pointe work. Exercises performed in pointe (toe) shoes.

Port de bras. Position of the dancer's arms.

Positions. There are five basic positions of the feet and arms that all ballet dancers must learn.

Retiré. Drawing the toe of one foot to the opposite knee.

Tendu. Stretching or holding a certain position or movement.

Tour en l`air. A spectacular jump in which the dancer leaps directly upward and turns one, two, or three times before landing.

Here's a look at what's ahead in STARS IN HER EYES, the third book in Fawcett's "Satin Slippers" series for GIRLS ONLY.

Leah pushed open the door to a small studio. She put down her soda, shoved her dance bag against the wall, then closed her eyes and tried to remember the steps to Princess Aurora's Act One variation. Slowly, thoughtfully, she proceeded to the left corner of the room. Then, humming the music very softly, she began to dance. Halfway across the floor she stopped. After the arabesque, then what? Leah shook her head and slowly sauntered back to her starting position. She stood lost in thought, her hands on her hips, trying to visualize the next combination of steps. She decided to try it from the beginning again. As she stepped into the opening arabesque, she heard a cough.

Leah gasped and looked behind her. "Oh! Miss Vreeland!" she cried, falling off pointe. Her hands flew up to her mouth.

"I'm sorry to disturb you," Lynne said, smiling.

"Disturb me?" Leah gulped. "Oh, no. You didn't disturb me. I shouldn't be here." She made a move toward the corner and her dance bag.

"Why not?" Lynne put down her own bag. "The only way you can become a really great dancer is to work at it every chance you get. *Every* chance," she emphasized. "But you look like you need a little help. Has Madame Preston taught you this variation yet?"

"No, we're learning the Rose Adagio but we haven't worked on the next part. I really haven't seen it since I was a kid, until today, that is."

"Let me show you." Lynne checked her delicate antique wristwatch, then began to mark the steps, naming them as she went.

Leah hung back only a second, but when Lynne looked at her in the mirror, she gained courage walked through the variation, following the lead of older dancer. She tried to match her movemen Lynne's. She was surprised how natural the step as she did them. Alex had always teased her tha was born to dance the role of Princess Aur *Sleeping Beauty*. After all, a variation from the last of the ballet had won her entrance into the Academy

"Now you try. I'll count." In a soft musical voice the ballerina counted and sang the melody. "Very good." She clapped as Leah finished the first sequence of steps. "I think the role suits you. Someday that's what the critics will say." Lynne looked at Leah carefully. "How old are you?"

"Fifteen. I'll be sixteen in May," she added somewhat apologetically. She felt terribly young in front of Lynne, and inexperienced and very far from being a great dancer. How had Lynne Vreeland become so sophisticated, so worldly?

A hazy look clouded Lynne's large blue eyes. "At your age I dreamed of dancing so many ballets." She ambled over to the barre and stared into the mirror. With her pinky she erased a smudge of mascara from beneath her eye. "But the role I wanted to dance most when I was a very little girl was Princess Aurora," she continued in a dreamy voice. "I saw Fonteyn dance it one time in New York. I was so little I hadn't even graduated to my first pair of toe shoes. But that's when I knew I wanted to be a ballerina someday. It's funny to think I'm still dancing that role."

A note of sadness crept into Lynne's voice. Leah looked at her carefully. At the moment, the great ballerina looked more like a slimmer, fit version of her own mother than a dancer portraying a sixteen-year-old.

... the first time in her life Leah realized how awful it ...st be someday to be too old for dancing. Her in-
... and ... reach out and comfort Lynne, but Leah
... f the ... g and awkward and didn't know how.
... ts to ... o dance was so foreign to her.
... s felt ... ed out the back of one leg, then suddenly
... t she ... Briskly she massaged the nape of her
... ra in ... ped Leah in a smile. Her smile was
... rm and sinc... e and oddly familiar. "I bet you'll get
... ance this role soon."

... ah gaped at the dancer. "Me?" she gulped.

... nne crossed the floor and rubbed some rosin on
... r hands, then ground the toe of each of her shoes in the flat wooden packing crate that served as the rosin box. "Yes, you," she stated firmly. "Madame Preston told me the school's spring gala performance will be *Sleeping Beauty*. From what I've seen of your dancing you won't have much competition for the role of Princess Aurora." Lynne looked at Leah critically and nodded her head before concluding, "Yes, you were really born for it."

Leah was speechless. Her head was swimming with the compliment. She felt shy, embarrassed, and overwhelmed. She looked down at the floor, over toward the piano, then toward the door. She fought the impulse to run out and tell Katrina or Alex or Linda exactly what Lynne had just said. One of the greatest ballerinas of all time thought she was born to dance the starring role in *Sleeping Beauty*.

ABOUT THE AUTHOR

Elizabeth Bernard has had a lifelong passion for dance. Her interest and background in ballet is wide and various and has led to many friendships and acquaintances in the ballet and dance world. Through these connections she has had the opportunity to witness firsthand a behind-the-scenes world of dance seldom seen by non-dancers. She is familiar with the stuff of ballet life: the artistry, the dedication, the fierce competition, the heartaches, the pains, and disappointments. She is the author of over a dozen books for young adults, including titles in the bestselling COUPLES series, published by Scholastic, and the SISTERS series, published by Fawcett.

SATIN SLIPPERS

The Lure of the Stage...
The Thrill of the Applause!

An exciting new GIRLS ONLY series that sweeps young readers into the heart and soul of ballet—from the glamour and romance of the stage to the incredible discipline, strength, and sacrifice required to get there.

Leah Stephenson, our young heroine, has studied ballet since she was four, and now at fifteen auditions for the San Francisco Ballet Academy. Thus begins her adventures as she performs for an audience for the first time, experiences jealousy and competition from the other dancers, and at the same time deals with her family, friends and school.